Praise for A Kind of Homecoming

Rose born and bred English, finds companionship and love with Sebastian, a German, in world sweetly unaware the Great War is about to erupt. As fate, or chance, steps in the story's perfect sense of place and characterization take hold. Excellent historical fiction.

- James Conroyd Martin author of *The Poland Trilogy*

A KIND OF HOMECOMING

BY GARY BAYSINGER

A Novella

C^2

See Square Press

ISBN: 978-0-578-28659-4 Print

ISBN: 979-8-218-03817-5 E-Book

Library of Congress Control Number 2022914610

See Square Press

Milwaukie, Oregon

Cover design by German Creative

Other books by Gary Baysinger

Margaret's Last Prayer

Available on Amazon.com
and
Garybaysingerauthor.com

For Mom and Dad

CHAPTER ONE

England, 1913

The shrill whistle pierced the quiet moments before the engine came into view. The string of cars came to a stop, followed by another blast from the horn. The arrivals exited the train, greeted by the smiles of their friends and family gathered on the platform. A young girl in a cream-colored dress—Rose guessed her to be about five—leapt into the arms of a silver-haired woman and said, "Gran, we're home." The two-dozen remaining people on the platform collected their bags, said their goodbyes, and shuffled toward the carriage.

Rose's mother embraced her, kissing her cheek.

"I'm proud of you."

A pang of longing jabbed at Rose's heart, and her feet failed to move her forward. She thought about what she would miss: accompanying her father on his rounds as he tended to sick animals, her mother's lectures on the importance of universal suffrage. Suddenly, the idea of leaving the warm comfort and security of home paralyzed her.

"Go on," her mother said. "This is your time."

Rose discreetly dabbed at her eyes, not wanting to

embarrass herself with a public display. She climbed aboard, finding a seat next to the window. Rose peered through the glass toward the platform, for one last look at Helen. The wrinkles around her mother's dark-brown eyes no longer visible, Rose imagined her mother, just for a moment, as a young girl in Scotland leaving home. The train shuddered to a start, the sign on the station slipping from view.

"Windermere," she whispered, caressing the words. The white and gray stone houses, half-covered in wisteria, faded away, disappearing behind the oak and ash trees. She'd traveled on the Windermere-Kendal line countless times, always looking forward to the outward journey, but reserving a mental space for the last leg of the return. Whether it was south to the coast or north to her grandparents in Scotland, the previous trips had been filled with anticipation of adventure, a break from the routine of a small Northern village. She collected stories about the busy cities and towns, stories she would tell her friends, which made the return trip deliciously sweet. But this trip was saying goodbye, turning the page on her childhood, making a new home. Windermere would always be special, but it would no longer be the destination.

"Where are you headed?" a voice asked. Deep in thought, staring out the window, she had taken no notice of the woman sitting across from her. Although dressed in a fine white linen blouse and dark-green skirt, Rose's attention was drawn upward to the enormous picture hat stacked with plumes of feathers. A lecture on the frivolous nature of feminine fashion and how it served only men's interests came to mind. "Don't put me on a pedestal," her mother once told her. "I prefer to stand on level footing."

Rose suppressed a smile before responding.

"Harrogate."

"Me as well. Taking in the waters?" the woman asked, spreading her empire hand fan to cool herself from the warmth of the carriage. It was a fair guess on the woman's part. Harrogate was known for the royal baths, and all that people of a certain social standing knew of the town was the Spa and the luxury hotels.

"No, I'm going to nursing school."

"Nursing school? How fascinating. A bit of adventure before you settle down. Good for you." The tone of the woman's voice, as she glided over the syllables, suggested anything but interest in Rose's choice of profession. Rose quickly put together a thumbnail sketch of her fellow passenger: a summer holiday in the Lake District, where she would take in the country air, then back to the social whirl in Manchester or London before boredom set in. Part of her wanted to enlighten the woman on the necessity of being independent, but her better angel won out.

"I hope so," Rose replied.

The woman smiled. "The first time I took in the baths, I met Tsarina Alexandra of Russia. I literally bumped into her on the street. Exquisitely dressed, ever so polite, flawless English. My husband refused to believe me when I told him."

Rose did her best to feign interest. She hated the English obsession with class. She steered the conversation to small talk about the weather and their families. Comfortable, safe, and boring. A small improvement. Rose learned the woman was visiting from Manchester, the other details instantly forgotten. The steam engine wheezed as the train climbed the gentle gradient, momentum slowing gradually until they crested the hill. Then the engine caught its breath and the train picked up speed as it slid eastward along the ridge.

Rose felt like she was on the roof of the world looking down on creation. The village appeared as a collection of dollhouses that could be rearranged to her liking. The post office, the pub, and school were indistinguishable now in the golden hue of the late summer sun. The Fells rose, slowly blocking out Windermere until it disappeared. She strained her eyes at the hillside overlooking the town, afraid that the moment had passed. Then she saw it, a cut of emerald-colored grass bleeding into the drab junipers. A little piece of land, it seemed so much bigger when you stood upon it looking down on the village below. Now, it was just a sliver disappearing behind the rise.

CHAPTER TWO

Germany, 1913

On his way back from Wissembourg, Sebastian met the Englishman who would alter his fate. It was easy to trace the connection between this chance meeting and how it shaped the arc of his life story.

His new Sunday routine was to pedal from the family farm to the outlying villages: Haguenau, Mertzwiller, Gundershoffen, all now within reach. The bicycle, a 1905 Victoria, was his pride and joy. He bought it for a bargain price from his neighbor Herr Huber, who had no use for it after his son moved to the city. Sebastian tinkered with it over the winter, fascinated by the interconnectedness of one part pushing or pulling another, immersing himself in the simple and complex design. But a bike—chain driven, two-wheels, powered by muscle—was more than just an object of fascination; it represented freedom. As his stamina increased, so did his range. The villages of Seltz or Munchausen, nestled along the River Rhine, became the goal for his nineteenth birthday in August, less than a month and a half away.

His thighs ached as he worked his way back,

emerging from the woods, high up on the ridge, the patchwork quilt of farms spreading out below him. In the distance, he could just make out the small cluster of houses and farms of his village. Estimating it would be another twenty minutes to home, he was already thinking about where he would go the following Sunday. Picking up speed on the slight downhill, back tire slipping on the gravel road, he negotiated the turn by deftly adjusting the front tire to keep the bike from spinning out from under him. Once around the bend, he noticed a man standing next to the side of the road, hands on hips, examining a motorbike.

Sebastian stared at the motorcycle. It didn't look like any of the German ones he'd seen before. The sloping handlebars and rakish tilt of the downtube gave it a look that spoke of comfort instead of function. So focused on this unfamiliar piece of machinery, he failed to see an enormous rut in the road. Suddenly, he was headfirst over the handlebars, landing with a crashing *thud*. It took a few seconds to get his bearings; his shoulder throbbed, his clothes were coated with dust, his palms stung from being scraped raw trying to break the fall.

"Are you hurt?" a voice called out. Sebastian was surprised to find the man standing over him with a look of concern on his dusty face.

Sebastian ran his hands over his chest, arms, and legs and, finding no further obvious injury, shook his head 'no.' The man reached out and pulled him to his feet.

"I'm relieved." He didn't sound like a Frenchman. He wore a heather-colored tweed suit with pant legs stuffed into full-length boots, and a pair of goggles resting above the visor of his matching flat cap. His face was dirty, save for the circles around his eyes. The fair complexion and blond hair peeking out from under his cap did not suggest Spanish or Italian. *Scandinavian or British*, Sebastian thought.

Sebastian brushed the dirt from his black trousers. "Thank you." Not accustomed to meeting foreigners other than nearby French, his curiosity got the better of him. "You are not German. Where are you from?"

"Is my accent that bad?" He pulled a card out of his breast pocket. "James Eadie, British."

Sebastian held the card in front of him, trying to decipher the English. One phrase leapt to his attention, *Enfield Motorcycles.* He looked back to the motorbike and the silver plaque above the V twin-engine, carrying the company's name. "You like the bike?" James said.

Sebastian blushed before meeting the man's gaze. "Forgive me. My name is Sebastian Maier. I live on a farm just down the road." He sneaked another glance at the bike. "Yes, I like motorcycles, cars, anything mechanical. I have heard about Enfield."

"Good news, I hope."

"Yes. One of the mechanics in Haguenau spoke highly of it. Better than anything the Germans or French could make."

"That's good to hear. But I'm afraid I'm not making a good showing of it now. The damn thing is not running."

"What's the trouble?"

"Well, it will run for a bit, then it sputters to a halt. I've had a look at it, but my skills are limited. You say you know a mechanic?"

"Yes, but Sunday is his day off." Sebastian circled the bike, surveying for any obvious problems. "Do you mind if I take a look?"

"Do you know motorcycles?"

"A little. I'm a self-taught mechanic."

James stepped back as if taking in Sebastian's full

measure. Sebastian's face became warm when he realized how preposterous his request must seem. *A farm boy in dirty work clothes and common labor shoes wants to tear your beautiful motorcycle apart because he's learned a few things about bikes.*

"Very well," he answered. "I don't have many other options, do I?"

Buoyed by this backhanded vote of confidence, Sebastian grinned. "I promise I won't damage your bike. I'm a good mechanic."

"There are tools in the left saddlebag," James told him.

Sebastian rubbed the dirt off his hands before he retrieved a pair of screwdrivers and several wrenches from the bag. He laid them out on the ground and walked around the motorcycle. He could feel the Englishman staring at him. Doubts crept into his mind. He'd only seen people work on bikes. It seemed easy when someone else did the work, but that was like singing harmony; now he had to solo. *Think logically*, he told himself. He recalled how the mechanics worked through a problem as he carefully pulled one part after another off the bike, examining for any mechanical defects, making a mental notation of where it came from. Everything appeared to be in working order. The solution didn't come, and he began to sweat, feeling he'd embarrassed himself by offering up his services.

The Englishman pulled out a cigarette and lit up. "Anything?" he asked.

"Nothing." Sebastian rubbed his jaw. "You say it will run, but it won't stay running?"

"Yes, and I've checked the gas tank too," the man replied with a hint of exasperation.

One last thing. He pried the fuel line off with a screwdriver. He blew into one end while holding his hand over the other. A faint whiff of air escaped. He squeezed the tube at one end, working his way toward the opposite end, finding a hard spot a third of the way down. He pressed and squeezed the object until it squirted out. It was a tiny twig, small enough that it would allow some fuel to pass, but not enough to keep the engine running smoothly. He held it up in triumph. "Here is your problem."

The Englishman grabbed the small piece of wood and examined it closely. Sebastian reattached the tube and the man climbed on the bike, kick-starting the engine. He waited, hearing no coughing, or sputtering, just a steady growl of internal combustion. The man grinned broadly as he switched the motor off. "Well done. I must say I had my doubts."

"I got lucky," Sebastian said.

"Can I buy you a drink?"

"A drink?"

"Yes, beer, wine, it's the least I can do. I'm sure you must know of somewhere nearby where we can get a drink."

"There's a Gasthaus just down the road a bit. It's not much. I know the owner."

"I'm not fussy. Point the way."

Sebastian gave directions and climbed on his bike, pedaling in the wake of the Englishman's dust. Ten minutes later, he leaned the bike up against the low fence surrounding the beer garden. The Gasthaus, a two story, half-timber affair with fading white paint, stood snugly up against a jumble of junipers, ferns, and birch trees. Half of the dozen tables inside the fence were occupied by neighboring farmers, some who greeted him by name as he made his way to where James sat reading a map.

"What are you drinking?"

"A beer."

James waved the proprietor down and Frau Oberman soon returned with two, tall, silver steins. "Prost," he said, raising his mug in salute to Sebastian. "You're a good mechanic."

"It's nothing. I've always been interested in mechanical things," Sebastian said.

"You've a real knack for it. I should know."

"How's that?"

James smiled. "My father owns the Enfield company. Co-owns, I should say."

"You're lucky, Mr. Eadie. What I would give to work on bikes like that."

"You don't want to stay on the farm?"

"No, I want to travel. See the world, learn things. My father says it's all the books I read. Mark Twain, Jules Verne. He says they put silly notions in my head."

James pulled his cigarette case out of his jacket pocket and offered one to Sebastian, who refused. Smoke swirled around them. "How would you feel about going to England?"

"England? I would like that. But I need to save money before I go anywhere."

"What if you had a job waiting for you?" James leaned in close. "As a motorcycle mechanic."

"I'm not a real mechanic. It's just something I do because it interests me," Sebastian said.

"You're a natural. You're better than most of the chaps I've seen." He tapped the ashes from his cigarette. "Motorcycles are new. If Enfield is to expand our business, we need more mechanics so people will be comfortable riding our motorcycles. I could set you up as an apprentice. You'd earn a living wage, have a chance to see God's own Earth. What do you say?"

It was as if the heavens had opened, shining their

light on Sebastian, his name pulled at random out of a hat. He'd dreamed of leaving the farm behind, but despite his scrimping and saving, it remained out of reach. Now, here it was right in front of him; he just had to grab it.

"How?"

"My father is well connected. A work permit would be a formality. Once you finish your apprenticeship, you could even move back to Germany, help us expand to the continent. Is that a 'yes'?"

Sebastian rubbed his jaw. "I'd need to talk to my parents first."

"Of course. You have my card. Write when you've made your decision. I'll smooth things over for you."

It was a lot to take in; his mind reeled at the thought of the opportunity. He'd never considered himself lucky and wondered if this stroke of good fortune belonged to someone other than him.

CHAPTER THREE

England, 1913

Rose fastened the top button on her coat as she headed out the door, running through her mental notations for the third time, or was it the fourth? The other nursing students chided her for being so tough on herself, but she wanted to impress the doctors with her knowledge. She repeated the Latin words for the muscles in the human hand as if it were a scripture. Lost in the nomenclature, her step off the curb onto Valley Drive hardly registered until a squeal of brakes pierced her thoughts. A bicyclist, eyes wide, white-knuckled, skidded toward her sideways. She drew in a breath, every muscle in her body tensing, bracing for the impact. At the last moment, the bike pivoted on its back wheel, the rider's shoulder passing within inches of her face. He swerved quickly left, then right, before pitching over in a clatter of metal on asphalt. Rose wobbled for a moment. She let out a gasp, breath hanging in the misty winter air. Horrified at being the cause of the accident, she rushed to help. The young man sat up on the damp street rubbing his ribs, muttering something unintelligible. Rose put a hand on his shoulder. "Are you alright? I'm dreadfully sorry, I've been so careless."

He looked up at her with a pair of the clearest blue eyes she'd ever seen. He tried to smile but with his lips pinched tight, it came off as more of a grimace. "Yes."

"I'm so sorry. I was not paying attention."

The man slowly rose to his full height, towering over her; she guessed he was six feet. He rubbed his slender frame once more before running his hands over his arms and legs. Seemingly satisfied, he picked up his cap and covered his mop of hair. Something was familiar; she searched her memory trying to place him.

"Charlie," she blurted out. The young man shot her a look. "You're my neighbor's friend."

Rose had been renting a room from Mrs. Bixby, a suffragist friend of her mother's. Charlie lived in the house next door. She had met this man once before, in passing, his name was Sebastian. There was some detail from their prior meeting she tried to remember.

"Yes, I'm a friend of Charlie. We met before," he replied in accented English.

German, that's it. The sound of his voice penetrated her thoughts, resonating in her head. "I thought so. I'm terribly sorry. I should be more careful. Are you sure you're alright?"

He smiled a crooked smile, nodded yes, and stared back at her.

"What about your bike?" she asked.

He turned his attention to the bike, picked it up, and made a quick inspection of the handlebars, the pedals, and the wheels. "Good, all is good."

"I'm sorry."

"Ach." He waived his scuffed hand as if to signal it was no trouble.

"I can help, I'm a nurse. Well, training to be a nurse." The blank look on his face told her that maybe he didn't completely understand.

He shook his head no, rooted to the spot, staring for a few seconds, before blushing and averting his gaze. "All is good."

He swung his leg over the bike, tipped his cap, and pedaled away. He shot a glance over his shoulder, offering the same charming smile. "Goodbye," he said, waving with his good hand. Rose watched him pedal away, her embarrassment subsiding just a little as he turned at the next intersection and disappeared. She wondered where he was off to before she remembered that Charlie told her they worked together in a bike shop. Maybe it was the excitement of the moment that clouded her senses, but something about this young man piqued her interest. She wondered how to discreetly inquire with her neighbors but changed her mind for fear it might appear too unladylike. Oh, but that smile.

CHAPTER FOUR

England, 1914

Sebastian walked downhill along Parliament Street with the loping stride of an athlete, passed the Royal Pump Room, turned left on Swan Road, and under the shadow of the handsome Edwardian buildings. He practiced his English out loud as the spring sunshine streamed down on him. "Would it be all right if I were to call on you?"

Upon arrival at the nursing college, he straightened his tie, patted the amulet in his vest pocket and took a deep breath. The woman at the front desk occupied her position with the confident air of a soldier in a well-defended position. A few wisps of gray hair had escaped from the bun at the back of her head, providing the only hint of contrast to her coal-black attire. She raised her eyes slowly, peering at him over her reading glasses.

"I am here to see Rose Maddox."

"Are you now?"

Her tone placed a seed of doubt in his brain. He'd not expected this type of inquiry. His pulse ticked up as she stared at him for several seconds before addressing him in nearly indecipherable English, "Who might you be?"

He explained himself and waited for the response, which came after a short pause. "Sit there," she said, pointing to the waiting room. He sat on the stiff wooden bench, fidgeting with his necktie again, twisting his fedora around. Rose, the young nurse he'd come to see, appeared in front of him with two other girls. He couldn't help but stare at her rosy cheeks and dark brown eyes.

"Sebastian, what a surprise!"

He shuffled to his feet and had to swallow the lump of nerves threatening to choke him. "I, uh, heard you moved."

"Yes, I did. I'm sharing a flat with another girl. It makes the rent much more affordable and she's good company."

"Uh, yes, that makes sense." He tried to think of some other bit of conversation while staring at his shoes as if he'd never seen them before, finding them an object of fascination.

"What brings you here?" she asked.

"I went to your house to see you and Charlie's mother told me you moved. I remembered that you worked … not worked … TRAINED to be a nurse. I asked for directions, and I am here." He stopped to catch his breath, relieved to have gotten the words right.

She nodded. "Yes, that explains how you came to be here. But why did you want to see me?"

His mouth felt coated with dust; the words forced out in a croaking sound. "Would it be all right if I were to call on you?" He looked back down at his shoes again for several seconds. When he looked up, Rose smiled, her warm eyes beaming at him.

"That would be lovely," she said.

The pressure he had heaped on himself, ever since he'd made up his mind to ask this question, lifted. An immense sense of relief swept over him. The tension driven out of his body, he stood for a long moment, unsure of what to do next. Part of him had not expected an affirmative answer. His face grew warm. Rose raised her eyebrows as if to indicate the next move was his.

"Oh, fantastic. May I ring you next Saturday at four?" he asked.

"Yes, that's fine, I'm free. Let me give you my new address."

Rose turned and walked to the registrar to borrow a pencil and paper. Sebastian stood awkwardly in front of the two other nursing students as they looked from him, then to each other. He dropped his hat, and then swooped to pick it up, grateful for the distraction. Rose returned and handed him a slip of paper.

"Next Saturday; I look forward to it."

"All is good then. Next Saturday," he said, awkwardly backing toward the exit.

In his haste to get away, before the girls could notice the red color seeping up his face, he turned without looking and walked right into a wall. A stabbing pain pierced his nose; his eyes watered as he staggered back a half step. He clamped his hand over his face, fearing that his nose was bleeding. Relieved to find no blood, he retreated outside, embarrassed and exhilarated at once. The sound of her classmates' laughter wafted out the open door with him.

One of the girls said, "I love his accent!"

Sebastian felt like his head was in the clouds as he made his way home.

***

The work week seemed to crawl by as he ticked the days off. When Saturday came at last, Sebastian dressed in his Sunday best: white shirt, three-button jacket, black pants, and black fedora, all of which served to make him look lean and lanky. He patted the amulet in his breast pocket for luck, rehearsing dialogue in his head, "I have two brothers and two sisters. How many brothers and sisters have you?" He tried to convince himself he was quick-witted and charming, moving the conversation along with a debonair ease.

He called on Rose at precisely four in the afternoon. She answered the bell wearing a lacy shirtwaist and a long narrow skirt that accentuated her slender figure. Her long, dark hair was pulled back. Her beauty intimidated him, but he hid his nervousness by focusing on being exceedingly polite.

"I thought we would go to the Harrogate Hydro for tea," he said.

"Lovely idea."

She stepped back inside, reappearing with a straw pioneer bonnet. They moved out to the sidewalk. Sebastian glanced around nervously before fixing his gaze on Rose.

"Where is the ...?" he stumbled, unable to remember the English version of the word, he resorted to French. "Chaperone."

"My mum told me I'm old enough to live on my own. I can take care of myself. She told me, 'Let the boys bring their own.'"

"Your father?"

"Oh, he went along with Mum. You have to know my mother. She's different."

Sebastian didn't fully understand the significance of Rose rolling her eyes, but he gathered that it was important. They walked to the Hydro in awkward silence as Sebastian unsuccessfully tried to recall some of the clever bits of conversation he'd rehearsed. The lack of a chaperone had thrown his rhythm; he'd expected a dialogue between three people, not two. It was like he was on a high wire without a net, in danger of crashing to the earth with a single misspoken word.

The Hydro was a gray-bricked Victorian building. Ivy trailed up to the second floor, giving it an air of class above anything he'd seen growing up in the Alsace countryside. Doubts began to creep in about the wisdom of his decision to come to this place. Inside, the ivory-colored walls and ecru linen tablecloths contrasted sharply with the dark furniture and hardwood floors, the high windows allowing the sun to spread a golden hue over the main room. Rose and Sebastian were seated at a table in the solarium. In an adjacent room, a white-haired man dressed in a navy-blue suit played Chopin on the baby grand. The well-dressed patrons spoke an English softer and more refined than what he was used to hearing at the garage, giving off a well-bred ambiance, making him feel like an imposter.

"You look nice," he said, as he pulled out her chair.

"Thank you. And you as well." The waiter appeared, handing them menus. Sebastian nearly gasped at the prices, discreetly patting his pocket to make sure he'd brought his wallet. He glanced over at Rose, watching her dark eyes absorb the words on the page. Backlit by the sun, her skin looked exquisite, like something out of a painting. He told himself to stop staring but felt like he was being pulled into an irresistible orbit—he liked the sensation. The waiter's return broke the spell. Sebastian ordered buttered scones and green tea, the cheapest item on the menu, quietly exhaling when Rose ordered the same thing. He asked her about her childhood, losing himself in the sound of her voice as he carefully picked out the words.

She said, "I grew up in the Lake District, where my

father is a veterinarian. I would often make rounds with him; I know all about cats and dogs and cows and pigs. Dad was forever being called away at all times of the day to tend to a sick calf or sheep."

"You make it sound hard."

"Taking care of animals is a lot of work, but something about the healing process appealed to me. Fixing something that's broken, making it whole. I like that," she said.

"Is that why you want to be a nurse?"

"Yes, I suppose so. People are easier to deal with. You talk to them, and they tell you what's wrong. My father told me I'd make a great doctor and tried to convince me to go to medical school in Edinburgh, but I thought it would be too hard. Tell me about your upbringing."

Sebastian confessed. "I grew up on a farm in Alsace, close to the French border."

"Oh dear, and here I'm saying how hard farm life is."

"It is much work. I became a little bored as well. I was more interested in mechanical things: motor cars, bicycles, those types of things. I like taking things apart and putting them back together. Fixing things, like you."

"How did you end up here?"

"It is a long story. A year ago, I was riding my bicycle when I came upon a motorbike broken down by the side of the road." He told her the story of meeting James Eadie. The waiter arrived with a tea cart, loaded with a silver caddie carrying a plate of buttered scones, small saucers of jam, and clotted cream. Sebastian watched as Rose poured the tea through a strainer and put a spoonful of sugar in her cup, stirring it back and forth. Wary that his manners might be lacking, he followed her lead and swirled his tea around and around, sloshing just a bit on the saucer. "I told Mr. Eadie I wanted to travel. He helped me to come work for Enfield. Here I am in Harrogate, working as an apprentice mechanic at Mr. Shaw's garage." He set his cup down. "At the garage, I met your neighbor, Charlie. His mother liked me and would invite me over for supper. I was traveling to his house when you passed me and said hello. Then, I saw you again."

"You mean you nearly ran into me."

"Yes, I'm sorry." His face went warm.

"I'm only teasing, I was the one at fault," she said.

"My English was no good, I was afraid to speak. I am better now," he said.

Rose said, "Yorkshiremen have a strong accent. Even other English people have a hard time understanding it."

"I have no problem with you."

"I don't mean to sound posh, but my mother was insistent her children spoke proper English."

"She did well."

"She also encouraged me to study French."

"*Tres bien*," Sebastian said. "*Je parle un peu*."

"*Vraiment* !" Rose replied. "Did you learn at school?"

"*Nein*, I mean no. We could not speak French at school. My grandparents spoke French at home when they didn't want us children to know what they were talking about. Alsace was part of France when they were young." Sebastian spread jam on his scone.

Rose asked, "Do you miss home?"

"I miss my mother's cooking and my family, but I want to travel. I read books by Twain, Kipling, and Jules Verne. My goal is to save money and go to America."

"What's so special about America?"

"I want to see the Wild West. Cowboys, Indians,

and, what's the word? Buffaloes."

She shook her head. "I'm not sure there are any real cowboys anymore."

Sebastian replied, "There is a little family history as well."

"What do you mean?"

He pulled a silver amulet out of his vest pocket. "Pay attention to this," he said, as he handed it to Rose.

She examined it closely. "A cross, set inside a heart, laid in a bed of roses. It's beautiful, where did it come from?"

"My grandfather Ernst wore it at the battle of Sedan when France lost Alsace to Germany. His grandfather, Jacob, wore it when he marched with Napoleon to Russia. Jacob had a brother who went to America; he wore a matching amulet. I want to find my American cousins. Opa Ernst said I would know them when I saw them," he pointed to the amulet in her right hand, "by this."

Rose raised her eyebrows. "That's quite a story. You should have a chain made so you can wear it."

"There is another twist … is that how you say it? Jacob had a comrade who lost the chain to his St. Christopher's medal at the battle of Borodino. He gave the man the chain from this amulet before the man died. After that, Jacob refused to replace it."

"The story just got better."

Sebastian shrugged. "I will have a chain made anyway."

"Really?"

"Yes, it is time to start a new leaf."

"Good for you, I think it's a splendid idea," Rose said.

Sebastian grinned. "Then we have an agreement, a new chain. All is good. Our first agreement."

She pursed her lips. "I didn't realize you were keeping track."

Sebastian's face grew warm.

Rose smiled. "You're blushing."

They both laughed, and his nervousness subsided. They finished their tea and walked back up Parliament Street, spending the rest of the afternoon wandering around the Stray and the Valley Gardens. He became at ease around her, his confidence in his English grew, and he lost track of time. Rose surprised him when she told him it was time for her to return home. They walked along Cold Bath Road, past the houses with the ornate slate-colored fences and black wrought iron gates, drawing to a stop in front of her flat. Sebastian took his hat off, holding it over his heart.

"Thank you; it was wonderful," he said slowly enunciating the words.

"Yes, it was," she said.

A moment passed before Sebastian stepped forward and opened the gate for her to enter the front yard of the building. He walked home, replaying the events of the day in his head, remembering the way she looked in the afternoon light, the way her eyes sparkled when she smiled. So engrossed in refreshing his recollections, he failed to notice he'd walked several blocks past his house.

CHAPTER FIVE

England 1914

They met again two weeks later, the rain giving way to a beautiful spring day, the sun highlighting the multiple green shades of the Yorkshire countryside. Sebastian had asked Rose to meet him in front of Shaw's garage with a head scarf and a pair of gloves. She arrived at half past five.

"I'm ready for my surprise," she said.

Sebastian said, "It was your nineteenth birthday yesterday."

"How did you know that?"

"Charlie told me. I have a gift for you."

Rose protested, "Oh no, you can't—"

"Wait," he held up his hand and hopped over to the corner of the garage, pulling the tarp off a Royal Enfield motorcycle with a sidecar.

"Charlie and I pulled it out of the River Knidd. We fixed it, also painted it. I would like to ride you around."

Rose circled the bike with a wary look in her eye. "I don't know, I've never been on a motorbike before," she said. "Is it safe?"

"Yes."

"What do I do?"

"You hold on."

Rose giggled. "Alright, let's go."

She tied the scarf around her head, slipped on the gloves, gathered up her skirt, and with Sebastian's assistance, climbed into the sidecar. The engine growled to life. They rolled out of the garage and within minutes were out in the countryside, blasting down the narrow lanes toward Menwith Hill. Sebastian cycled through the gears in a fluid motion, keeping the engine running with a steady whine as they went up and down the dales. Between the villages of Hampsthwaite and Darley, a farmer wearing Wellington boots and a tweed flat cap stood in the middle of the road, holding his hand up to signal them to stop.

Sebastian slowly brought the bike to a stop ten paces from the man and cut the motor. The farmer turned to his right, signaling to a younger man by the side of the road who opened a wooden gate in the stone fence. A flock of sheep burst out from behind the wall, herded across the road by a pair of collies, as the older man whistled commands. A mass of wool swarmed past the Enfield and sidecar. The earthy smell of the animals burrowed into Sebastian's lungs, the bleating sound drummed into his brain, reminding him of home. He wondered if she felt the same primal connection. Rose reached over and put her hand on Sebastian's forearm; a pleasant tingling sensation raced from his elbow to his heart.

"This is a wonderful present. Thank you."

***

Rose and Cora had become friends from the first day at nursing school. Cora had been raised near the village of Wetherby and the two of them bonded over a mutual desire not to return to life in a country village.

After her first outing with Sebastian, her friend pressed for details about the day's events. She expressed surprise after she found that Rose went without a chaperone, nodding her grudging approval when informed that the young man in question acted appropriately.

Rose sat at the table in the small anteroom the students used for tea breaks. As the kettle whistled its finish, she prepared herself for the line of questioning that was sure to follow. Cora entered shaking her blonde head. "Mrs. Hughes, I swear her job is to make my life miserable."

"Do I want to know?" Rose asked.

"No, ignorance is better."

Cora sat across from her, stirring sugar into her steaming cup.

"All right Miss Maddox, full story, let's hear it."

Rose recounted the details of the ride while Cora narrowed her eyes as if trying to read between lines, looking for a clue.

"That's all that happened?"

"Yes, that's all."

"He didn't try to kiss you, didn't try to put his hands on you?"

"No, he was a perfect gentleman."

"What's wrong with him?" Cora asked.

"Pardon?"

"I'm suspicious; he didn't try anything."

"What are you talking about?" Rose sputtered. "Last time you were worried he might do something, and now you're saying he should."

"No, I'm not saying he should. I just expected it. Being a foreigner and all that. You know how those Germans can be. All hands, from what I hear."

"Where did you hear that?"

"Word gets around."

"You mean a rumor," Rose said.

Cora shrugged her shoulders, sipping her tea as if to signal a change in the conversation.

"Will you see him again?"

"Yes, he wants to take me out next Sunday, to York."

"Are you going?"

"Yes, I don't see why not. He's nice."

Cora made a clucking sound, looking away for a moment.

"What now?" Rose asked.

"You should have said no. Make him work a little harder."

"Why would I do that?"

"You don't want him to think you're an easy catch. You could have told him you have another fella calling on you. That would fix him."

Rose laughed. "Are you trying to be my friend?"

"I only want what's best for you, dear."

"Thank you."

"So, he's the one?" Cora asked.

"We've only seen each other twice."

"Now you're telling lies. I can see it in your eyes, you fancy him."

Rose felt her face flush. "I ... I"

"That settles it."

"Stop it, I do like him, just not like you think I do."

Cora rolled her eyes and appeared to suppress a smile. "Your secret is safe with me, love."

"You're incorrigible."

"You'll thank me later. I do like his accent."

***

Their romance blossomed as the weather warmed and the days grew longer. They soon developed a routine: Sebastian would wash up after work, grab the Enfield, ride to her flat, and they would roar down the quiet country lanes to the nearby villages of Pateley Bridge, Knaresborough, and Ripon. On the second Saturday of June, they rode to Bolton's Priory, exploring the ruins on foot. They followed the riverbank that nearly encircled the grounds, coming to a grassy slope between the River Wharfe and the ancient cemetery in front of the Abbey. Standing at the top of the banks, they looked up at the exposed oval arches forming the ribs of the tenth-century monastery.

Rose said, "The abbey was built over a thousand years ago …."

Sebastian heard the words, but they didn't register. His heart pounded, and his hands shook as he turned toward her. Something about the way her lashes fluttered and danced above her dark eyes filled him with yearning unlike anything he had experienced before.

"… Scottish raiders in the mid-fourteenth century …"

He took a deep breath. The drumbeat of his pulse grew louder, urging him on until he leaned in and kissed her. A sensation of lightness overcame him, as if he was in danger of drifting away. Everything stopped; the rest of the world receded into the background. All he could feel was his heart doing the St. Vitus dance. When he opened his eyes, the smile on her face went straight to his brain; he felt like he was floating on air. The rest of the day went by in a blur. Later, when he dropped her back at her flat, he could not recall any part of their conversation. All he could think of was how long until the next time he saw her. He prayed he'd not said anything that would come back to haunt him.

***

Cora was right: he was the one. Rose's time with Sebastian became a precious commodity, something to look forward to after a hard day at school. Their lives intertwined like a couple of vines; her days filled with thoughts of their last visit. When she was with him, she wanted to hold back the hands of time, stretching out the moment. She felt it in her bones, they were destined to be together. But as much as she wanted to believe, a tiny reserve of doubt harbored in the back of her mind, a voice of caution. Although her mother had raised her to be independent, Helen's approval would validate her instincts. There was only one way to find out: take him home to Windermere.

In July, they made a mid-week trip to the Great Yorkshire Show in Bradford, a show about farm animals and farm equipment. Rose laughed, thinking about how these were the very things she wanted to leave behind. But Sebastian was keen on going, and she viewed it as an opportunity to ask him for a visit to her parents. On the ride over, she tried to suppress her anxiety by rationalizing it as just another outing on the motorbike, but her own lies were unconvincing. When they arrived, she bought a bag of popcorn to distract herself. Sebastian seemed at ease, in his element, easily engaging the taciturn Yorkshire farmers, talking about gear ratios on tractors and the latest developments in plowshares. The depth of her feelings for him deepened. "I'm impressed. That's a tough crowd to win over," she said.

"Oh, we talk farm life; it is the same in Germany."

Her face went warm. "How would you feel about

coming up to my parents' place in the Lake District this weekend? I was planning on taking the train, but I thought it would be much more fun on your bike. We could leave after work on Friday and get there before dark." Her hands became cool and moist, she rubbed them together, but stopped herself for fear of how silly she might look. The corners of his mouth slowly turned upward; his pale blue eyes seemed to smile.

"Yes, that would be nice," he said.

She exhaled, telling her heart to be still. This leap of faith stirred something inside her, filling her with gladness.

"Perfect, I'll let Mum and Dad know."

CHAPTER SIX

England, 1914

On Friday, Sebastian showed up at the nurse's college shortly after noon. After a brief interrogation by Miss Brown, the Scottish registrar, he was told to wait in the sitting room. He could feel her staring at him as he walked away. Rose appeared a few minutes later.

"Sebastian, you're lucky you caught me, I was at lunch. Is there something wrong?"

"No, I have a surprise," he said. "Charlie has a new camera, a Kodak. It's American. He took a photo of the bike we worked on." Sebastian held up the gray camera case.

"I see," Rose said, with a puzzled look on her face. "It looks like a lady's handbag. You came here to show me that?"

"No, I want your photo."

"In my nursing uniform?" Rose said. "Why don't we do this when I can put on some nice clothes?"

Sebastian explained. "The first time I saw you, you had on your nursing uniform. My mother told me, 'Remember the small moments.' I want a souvenir."

Rose hesitated, doubt flickering in her dark-brown

eyes.

Sebastian said, "It will take only a minute. If you do not like it, we throw the photograph away."

"Okay, but I get the final say."

"Of course," he said. "We can go outside; the light is good there."

Sebastian unsnapped the button, unfolding the camera from the case. He adjusted the settings as Rose sat on the low wall separating the nursing school grounds from the sidewalk, folding her hands on her lap.

"Hold," he said, steadying the camera. "Smile," and clicked the shutter.

He put the camera back on the saddlebag of the bike, then came and stood next to her. "I have to go back. I will see you later today."

As he kissed her goodbye, he could hear a young woman serenading from the upstairs window. A blonde girl leaned her head out of the window above, "*I saw Rose and her fella under the apple tree, k-i-s-s-i-n-g.*"

Rose looked up. "Thank you, Cora," she said with a smirk. The blonde girl stuck her tongue out.

"A friend?"

"No, a madwoman." Her inviting smile left him rooted to the spot. She laughed, giving him a gentle nudge. "Go back to work."

***

That evening, Sebastian carefully fastened their bags to the back of the bike and he and Rose took off, traveling the winding back roads, through the patchwork quilt of farms and small streams. They skirted the Yorkshire Dales, slowing only in small villages where they drew long looks from the inhabitants. As the sun began to set, the visage of the Fells rose up before them, slightly unfocused in the lengthening shadows. Twenty minutes later, they passed a small village with a sign that read "Windermere" and pulled up in front of a thatched cottage with wisteria climbing toward the second-story windows.

A red-headed boy in short pants scurried across the street and gawked at the bike. Sebastian smiled at him as he unloaded their bags.

Rose said, "Hello, Tommy. How are you?"

"I'm fine, Miss Maddox."

"Sebastian, this is Tommy, my neighbor. I went to school with his older sister."

Tommy looked at the bike, then at Rose, and then at Sebastian, as if weighing something in his mind. "Is this your fella?"

She laughed. "Yes, I suppose he is."

The ease at which the words flowed over her lips illuminated Sebastian's heart like a flame. He lost himself in the glow of that idea until he realized conversation had stopped and Tommy was focusing on something behind him. Sebastian followed his gaze to the bike and knew exactly what the lad wanted. "Tommy, tomorrow," he said, pointing to himself and back to the boy, "would you like a ride on the bike?"

The boy's eyes lit up. "Yes, please."

Sebastian put the bags down and held out his hand for the boy to shake. "Tomorrow," he repeated solemnly. He picked up the bags and followed Rose through a low wooden gate to the front entrance of the house.

A plaque next to the door read:

J.V. Maddox
M.R.C.V.S.
Veterinary Surgeon

Rose paused, turning to Sebastian.

"I must warn you my parents are a little different."

"Different?"

She frowned. "Some people consider them unusual. They call themselves progressives. It's my mother; she does not agree with the status quo, she thinks there's a double standard for women. Mum is the head of the local chapter of the National Union of Women's Suffrage."

"Suffer? I don't understand."

"They believe that women should be treated as equal to men, that women should be able to vote."

A light switched on in his head. "Oh, yes, there is a progress party in Germany. They want the same."

"She also likes to paint in her spare time and considers herself an artist. Her dream is to visit the Louvre in Paris."

He nodded. "I understand. An artist, painting, museum."

"And don't mention anything about the Malthusian League." She rolled her eyes. "Mother had a falling out with them."

"What league?"

She looked him up and down before her dark eyes met his gaze. "Never mind. Just be yourself."

That feeling of seeing himself in her eyes thrilled Sebastian, sending a warm, pleasant feeling all the way to his toes. He had to collect his thoughts before replying, "I hope that is so."

When Rose shoved open the solid, oak door, a Cocker spaniel and a King Charles spaniel rushed at them barking and jumping up and down. The dogs greeted Rose with wagging tails, bumping their shoulders against her legs. "That's Joey and the little one is Jade." The dogs eyed him with suspicion as she led the way through the sitting room and surgery to the kitchen. A faint smell of ether hung in the air. Her parents, James and Helen Maddox, rose from the table and swept their daughter up in hugs. Her father had thinning, brown hair and wore dark flannel trousers and a white shirt with a fraying collar. Sebastian could see Rose had inherited her mother's warm brown eyes and thick, dark hair. They greeted Sebastian enthusiastically, immediately putting him at ease. James announced he was just on his way to the chip shop, throwing on his jacket on his way out the door. Rose gave a quick tour of the house and practice, wrapping up just as her father returned with hands full of grease-stained newspapers. They crowded around the kitchen table as the smell of fried cod and vinegar permeated the room.

Helen said, "So you're from Germany."

"Alsace. I grew up on a farm near the River Rhine. I am here one year now."

"I'm sure your mother misses you."

"Every letter asks for when I come home."

"You're her son. She'd swaddle you in cotton if she could," Rose said.

He had no idea what the last part of that sentence meant so he smiled and said, "I am going for a visit soon."

"Really?" Helen said.

"Yes, I have saved for a steamer to Rotterdam. From there, I can get a boat down the Rhine to Heidelberg. A train to home."

James said, "That'll make your mum happy."

Helen asked, "Do you plan to return to the farm someday? I mean, permanently?"

"I do not think so. I am happy that I lived there, but I want to travel and try new things."

Helen smiled, "No more getting up at dawn to milk cows. No more standing in the freezing cold during calving season, no more mud." She shot a sideways glance at her husband.

James chuckled at her depiction of farm life. "The life of a veterinarian. The great outdoors, sunshine, and fresh air."

"Don't forget the horse manure and having to stick your arm up some cow's backside," Helen said. Everyone laughed.

CHAPTER SEVEN

England, 1914

The next morning, as the sun burned through the mist covering the hills, rays of light filtered through the small window in the kitchen. Sebastian had already eaten by the time Rose joined him at the table, but he was content just to be in her presence, happy to talk about her dogs and the weather. After breakfast, she said, "I'd like to take you to one of my favorite places. How do you feel about a picnic?"

"Yes, good idea."

"It's a bit of a hike, but I think you'll like it."

Rose grabbed an old knapsack from the closet, and they packed bread, cheese, hard boiled eggs, and a small blanket. They stepped out into the sun and followed the road south through the village, passing an eighteenth-century inn with hydrangea bushes climbing the trellis. Rose pointed to a slate-gray stone building across the cobblestone alley from the inn. "That's the primary school where I learned my letters."

On the edge of the village, an old man in rumpled clothing, sitting on the bench in front of the post office, tipped his flat cap. "Morning, Miss Rose."

"Good morning, Mr. Kennerly. How are you?"

"Right as rain. Waiting for Jack."

"That's good," she said, without breaking stride. Sebastian stared at the man, who took no notice of him.

A hundred paces down the road, Rose turned to Sebastian and sighed. "It breaks my heart."

"What?"

"That's old Mr. Kennerly; he used to own one of the big farms here in the parish. His only child, Jack, was killed fighting in South Africa thirteen years ago, in the Boer War." She turned to look over her shoulder. "He comes to town once a week to meet the bus, but Jack never comes home."

Down the road, they came to a pier that jutted into Lake Windermere. A dozen people waited as a small steamer ferry, *The Tern*, moored up to the pier. They paid their fare, boarded the old wooden boat, and puttered to the Western shore. Twenty minutes later, they approached a cut in the tree line, revealing an old pier and the road leading to the village of Fur Sawrey. The passengers disembarked, Rose and Sebastian turning north on the country lane. Stone walls draped with blackberry bushes edged the road. They took a footpath past the Baileys' farm, whose fields were dotted with little white clouds of Herdwick sheep, reaching the foothills of the Fells. They climbed a winding path up the hill, passed a crumbling, two-story octagonal-shaped tower, and continued through a tangle of spruce and pine trees. He admired her graceful stride as she forged uphill at a brisk pace, and he worked to keep up.

After two hours of hiking, Rose led them down a narrow deer trail, ducking under and stepping over low-hanging branches and fallen trees. Red squirrels scattered at their approach, chattering to one another as they scampered away. Ten minutes later, they came to a small clearing covered in lush meadow grass, with a view of the village below nestled between the blue-gray waters of the lake and the green wooded hills. A gentle breeze carried the scent of pine.

"This is the place. What do you think?" she asked.

Sebastian surveyed the scene. "Fantastic! It is like the Vosges mountains," he said, looking at Rose standing under the noonday sun. "I love it."

Rose said, "I like to think of it as my own special place. I found it by accident when I was hiking one summer. It's like a private room with a view."

She pointed to the lake. "That's Belle Isle, the big one."

Sebastian dropped the knapsack, pulled out the blanket, and handed it to Rose. She carefully spread it on the ground. "Take your shoes off, please; we don't want to track dirt on the blanket."

"Of course," he said, removing his boots and stepping on the blanket, where his stockinged feet touched hers. He realized that this was the first time the two of them had been completely alone together. A pang of desire tugged at him. He took her in his arms and kissed her. Through her damp blouse, he could feel her body relax as he ran his hands down to the small of her back. They stumbled, collapsing back on to the blanket, laughing with giddy nervousness. That feeling of the world revolving around him came over him again. The azure sky, the verdant meadow, and the bird calls all faded as he kissed her. He savored the feeling, drinking in the sunshine as the afternoon rays blanketed the valley like a shawl, filling him with a sense of wonder. They lay under the shelter of the Northern sky, saying little to one another. He wanted to just be in the moment, as if conversation would break the spell. She pulled back, propping herself on her elbows.

"Hungry?"

"Yes."

She unpacked the rucksack, spreading out the food on the edge of the blanket. They ate in silence, looking across the quiet valley as a melody of unspoken words filled the space between them. When they finished, he lay back and Rose curled next to him, head resting on his chest while humming a tune he didn't recognize. Life seemed easy, effortless almost. He closed his eyes for a moment, trying to imagine a future for the two of them, what it could look like, wondering if it was naïve to think such a thing was possible. Then he imagined what it would be like to be with her, to share a moment of intimacy. He'd no experience with carnal pleasures and the simple idea of his flesh pressing against hers aroused a tingling sensation all over his body. He didn't want to fight the feeling; he wanted to swim in it, let it cover over him. He woke to Rose nudging him on the shoulder, his face flushed at the thoughts he harbored without her knowledge. It felt like he crossed an unspoken boundary. An apology seemed in order. "I'm sorry. I was sleeping."

She leaned over, smiling down at him. "I hated to disturb you, but I'm getting warm. Your face is red; you've had a bit of sun."

Sebastian felt relieved, happy she could not read his thoughts. He sat up, stretching his arms. "To be like today, every day, would be good."

"*Parfait*," she said.

They packed away the remains of the picnic and shook out the blanket. Sebastian, intoxicated on the sensual pleasure of the afternoon, felt his inhibitions slip away. "What would you think of a trip to Whitby next weekend? Charlie told me of a small inn that is nice, and not too much money. He knows the owner; we can get two rooms cheap." He held his breath waiting for her response, knowing that his request bordered on the risqué. He hoped he had judged right but feared he might have overplayed his hand.

"Two rooms?" she replied, drawing out the words while holding him in her gaze. Her irises became darker, almost shiny, and the corners of her mouth turned upward to reveal a trace of a smile.

"Yes, of course," he said, trying to push away the impure thoughts coming to his mind.

"Well, I think it's a terrific idea. I've always wanted to go."

The thought of the two of them spending the night under the same roof, unchaperoned, left him exhilarated, and a little frightened.

***

Tommy waited for them when they returned to the house. Sebastian waved as they drew near. "Yes, time for your ride." Tommy climbed into the side car, looking expectantly at the two young lovers. "Ready?" Sebastian asked as he started up the bike, gunning the motor, laughing at the young lad's obvious excitement. It reminded him of his own passion for bikes, cars, and motorcycles. He took the boy up and down the street in second gear, revving the engine high, attracting the attention of the townspeople, all to the delight of Tommy, who smiled, laughed, and waved at the people they passed.

That evening, they sat around the kitchen table playing dominoes. Sebastian and Rose tried to act as casual as possible but exchanged surreptitious glances at one another while touching hands under the table. James and Helen talked about gardening and the season's harvest.

James said, "Your English is quite good."

"Oh, it's not so good; I'm still learning."

"Did you know any English before you came to Britain?"

"A little: please, thank you, how much, where is this located. Before I came to Britain, one of my old teachers gave me a German-English phrase book and dictionary. I study every night, write, talk, and get a little bit better. Then I read English newspapers, mark the words I don't understand."

James said, "So you are informed on current affairs."

"Yes, a little."

For a moment, Sebastian thought there would be discussion of the possibility of war. The chatter about what the Austro-Hungarians would do, and who would fight, made for bigger headlines every day. His heart told him that a diplomatic solution would be reached, but he couldn't ignore the buzz in his head telling him that Germany would be drawn in to the conflict. He felt relieved as they focused on their tiles and the moment passed. He didn't want to think about war, not now.

Helen asked her daughter. "What time do you think you can get to the cottage?"

Rose replied, "Monday afternoon, I should think."

Helen turned to Sebastian, "Did Rose tell you we're headed to the beach in Brighton next week? We go there every summer."

This was the first Sebastian had heard of it. "Yes, that is nice."

Rose glanced at him and squeezed his hand. The four of them played until midnight, when James announced it was time to turn in and everyone retired to their respective rooms.

As Sebastian was preparing for bed, Rose knocked on the door and entered his room.

He said, "You are missing your family holiday?"

"Let me explain," she said, wrapping her arms around him. "I was originally scheduled to be on duty at the hospital that Sunday. So, I told my mum and dad that I would have to come down on Monday. I just found out yesterday that I've been taken off the schedule. I was going to tell them, but you asked me to Whitby. Brilliant, I thought. I'll go to Whitby and then Brighton on Monday. I wanted to see you before your trip home."

Sebastian ran his fingers through her hair. "I would like that as well." That familiar tingling sensation came over him as he thought about how next weekend might play out.

"Mostly, I wanted you to myself before any of those *frauleins* tempt you to stay."

He chuckled. "You would be like the siren Lorelei, calling me back." He gave her a tender kiss. "Tell me about Brighton."

"We've been going ever since I was a baby. It's a long train journey. We rent a cottage near the beach, swim in the ocean with Dad, and walk the boardwalk. Mother paints me and my brother. If you look through her work, you can see us growing up. You can also see what phase she was going through. She would get books from the library and read about the lives of painters like Matisse, and Gauguin. She'd read about their styles of painting and try them out on our portraits. One year I was done in the style of Monet, the next da Vinci."

"What about van Gogh?" Sebastian said.

"Yes, there was the van Gogh year."

"Did you have two ears?"

"Don't be daft." She kissed him on the cheek. "Good

43

night."

CHAPTER EIGHT

England, 1914

Rose woke early, dressed, washed her face, and made her way downstairs, where she knew mother would be waiting. Helen, no matter what activities had gone on the night before, was always the first one up. Quite often, it was to prepare breakfast for Rose's father before his rounds, or a sandwich in case he was called out in the middle of the night. Rose had a hard time reconciling her mother's talk of independence with the way she fawned over her husband, even though Helen, always ready with an answer, had explained it years earlier. "I do it because I want to, not because I feel I have to."

Rose pushed open the door to the scullery, and found her mother sitting at the kitchen table, staring into her teacup as if looking for an answer to something, the muted light, softening her profile.

"Morning, Mum."

Helen smiled. "Morning, sunshine. Tea?" She pushed back her chair.

"I'll get it, Mum."

Rose fixed a cup and joined her mother at the

simple, white oak table, where food was prepared, and small meals eaten. The dining room, with its formal appearance, was used for big meals and for entertaining guests. It was more suited for discussions on politics and literature, subjects with a scholarly feel, topics that would remain there until the next meeting. The kitchen felt more intimate, a place where you could let your guard down and be more personal. She wondered how many conversations had taken place here, how many secrets were sunken in the grooves etched into the surface. She could run her fingers along the contours like a blind person and know the story of the family. Rose waited for the questions that were sure to come.

"I didn't know what to expect, but he's nice," Helen said.

Rose sighed. Her mother's response validated her feelings for Sebastian. "Yes, he's very sweet."

"Are you in love with him?"

The directness of the question caught her off guard. Rose felt her face grow warm before she regained her composure. "I am not sure. How would I know if he is the one? I've had other boys fancy me, but …"

"But you're not a little girl anymore, and Sebastian is not a school-boy. He's a young man. It's different."

"I know, it's just that …"

"What?"

Rose said, "I can't describe it. Growing up here in this little village, I always wanted to get away, to see other places. Now, I am away at school. I've met a young man, a foreigner, and the opportunities to get out to find something new and different are standing right in front of me. Yet, I'm afraid I'll make the wrong choice and end up unhappy."

Helen said, "None of us know if the decisions we make today will lead us to happiness tomorrow. Events sometimes overtake us. You must trust yourself, follow the light within your heart, let it be your guide."

"Mother, were you afraid when you left Edinburgh to come to this country village? It couldn't have been easy to leave your home behind and start over."

"Home is not just a location. It's who you share your life with. I came here because your father accepted me for who I am. He never asked me to change. I knew the two of us could build a life together, I'm not talking about bricks and mortar, we built this home with our love."

Rose didn't know what it meant to be in love or how to distinguish it from childish infatuation. In the last few months, Sebastian had taken up a place in her life, deep in her heart. The thought of his absence unsettled her; a picture of the future without him looked dark. She was relieved when her mother changed the subject.

"How was your hike yesterday?"

"It was great, a perfect day for it."

Her mother smiled broadly before taking another sip of tea.

"What are you smiling at?"

"Nothing, I know that place is special, and you wouldn't take just anybody. I think you've answered the question I asked earlier."

Rose tried to downplay the importance of the occasion in her mind, but she couldn't. "I suppose you're right."

"Enjoy yourself; life is short," Helen said.

***

On the return trip that afternoon, Rose and Sebastian were a few miles from Harrogate when the dark clouds that had threatened rain all morning finally delivered.

He shouted over the roar of the motor, "Halt?"

She shook her head no. "Keep going, we're almost there."

They soldiered on through a hail of raindrops, heads down, water pelting them, soaked through when he dropped her off at her flat.

"I had a wonderful weekend," she said, as a drop of rain slipped down her nose.

"Me too. Thank your parents; they were fantastic." He kissed her, pulled away from the curb, and roared off down the street.

***

On Friday, Rose went to Ogden's Jewelers on James Street and placed an order for a necklace to match Sebastian's amulet. Mr. Ogden assured her it would be ready by the first week of August. She walked out with a bounce in her step, the recklessness of her love lifting her higher than she'd ever been. Immersed in her own world, she failed to notice Sebastian crossing the street directly behind her and entering the jeweler's.

CHAPTER NINE

England, 1914

On the last Saturday in July, Rose and Sebastian left Harrogate at mid-morning, heading east toward the North Sea coast. After a tour of the village of Darrowby, they were soon out on the North Yorkshire moors. The blazing sun blanketed the undulating fields of purple and red heather that stretched to the horizon. He didn't see Whitby until they were almost on top of it, the sides of the surrounding cliffs rising as they made their way down Church Street. He parked the bike in front of the town square on Market Place. The Greenlee Hotel occupied the west side of the square, sharing a wall with the Squinting Cat Public House. Sebastian found the English habit of giving their pubs peculiar names somewhat mystifying; it was like a joke he would never understand. The red front door and matching red poppies in the sill planters on the first- and second-floor windows lent a splash of brightness to the yellow bricks worn down by centuries of rain. Once inside, a common area with a fireplace led them to a teenage boy behind the front desk.

Sebastian and Rose stepped up to the desk and

placed their bags on the floor. Hoping to strike an authoritative tone, Sebastian asked, "I was told rooms are available?"

The boy said, "You'll have to speak to Mr. Greenlee about that; he's out to lunch. Back in 'bout an hour. You can leave your bags here if you want to have a look around."

Bags checked, they walked downhill to the river, crossing over the swing bridge to the northern half of the town.

"I'll miss your birthday next week," she said.

"Yes, I'm sorry, but Mother would be unhappy if I didn't come home for my birthday."

"I understand. I have a present for you when you come back."

"What is it?" he said.

"It's a surprise."

"Really, I have ways of making you talk."

"You don't know me very well; I'm tougher than you think."

He smiled at her, and she squinted back at him. They strolled the boardwalk as gulls soared overhead and parents eyed their children wading in the surf. He took in the smell of salt air mixing with popcorn before she stopped in front of Castell's Photographers Shop next to the curio.

"Let's get our picture taken."

Sebastian looked at the photographs on the wall. "Yes, good thought."

The proprietor, a portly, red-haired gentleman with a bowler hat and handlebar mustache, welcomed them heartily. "Oh aye, a photograph of the beautiful young couple," he said with relish. Laying on the charm he added, "You two look so nice I think I'll keep a copy on my wall as an advertisement."

They settled on a price, and he ushered them into the backroom with a large white canvas on the wall and a stool in front of it. The man motioned to Rose. "Ma'am, please have a seat. Sir, please stand behind her to the left." They moved into position as he adjusted the lights and began to set up his equipment.

"How long have you done this?" Sebastian asked.

The man made some adjustments to the camera. "Oh, about five years now. What I really wanted to be was a naval architect." He stepped back from the camera for a second and held the flash up.

Sebastian asked, "Is that true?"

"Yes, I wanted to work on bellybuttons." He laughed at his own joke, and they smiled back.

"Perfect," the man said, and the bulb flashed.

Sebastian gave him his address in Harrogate, and the man assured them that he would have the photographs delivered within a fortnight. They continued along the boardwalk, stopping at an arcade. Sebastian showed off his prowess with darts, winning a pair of costume jewelry rings. He ceremoniously placed one on Rose's finger and one on his own. They worked their way back to the hotel, passing a newspaper kiosk where the headlines shouted out Austria's ultimatum to Serbia. The smile fell away from her face, and the bounce seemed to go from his step.

"The war is coming, isn't it?" Rose said.

"The world is mad."

"You will be called up, won't you?"

"Maybe," he said, knowing full well he'd be drafted if the war came.

She tilted her head toward him. He wondered if his lie was so obvious there was no need to challenge it. A small untruth to give succor to both the deceiver and the deceived, a tacit understanding that this was protection against the hard edges of life. He took her hand, admiring the ring. Her gaze met his, and the look in her eyes he could only describe as desire, or a longing for something out of reach. They arrived back at the hotel and found a rosy-cheeked man with thinning blond hair and the stern nature of a Presbyterian minister occupying the front desk.

"You are Mister Greenlee?"

"Aye. What can I do for you?"

"Are there any rooms for the night? My friend Charlie told me you would have rooms."

Mr. Greenlee looked him up and down and said, "Yes, he did ring ahead. You're in luck, we've one room left." His eyes shifted to their cheap rings. "Perfect for the newlyweds."

The last comment confused Sebastian. *Newlyweds?*

"Thank you. We're on our way to Scotland for our honeymoon," Rose said.

At the mention of Scotland, Mr. Greenlee's face lit up. "Young master Charlie neglected to tell me that you were honeymooning. Congratulations! You'll have a great time in Scotland, wonderful place. I grew up near Aberdeen."

"Oh, we're so looking forward to it," she replied.

He smiled as he placed the register on the counter. Sebastian hesitated, no longer sure of his next move, wondering if his English comprehension had failed him.

Rose nudged his arm. "Go on, dear, sign us in as husband and wife. I know it takes some getting used to." He paused and looked at the pen in his hand as if he'd forgotten how to write. "Go on," she repeated.

He leaned forward and wrote *Mr. and Mrs. Maier, Harrogate, Yorkshire*. Rose smiled at Mr. Greenlee, and Sebastian wondered if they passed as newlyweds. The two of them walked up the steps to the first floor, grinning to one another and trying to suppress giggles.

"Did we just …?"

"Shh …" she said, placing a finger on his lips.

"Are you certain about this?"

She nodded. Sebastian smiled as he opened the door to their room, and then without warning, swept Rose off her feet and carried her across the threshold. She squirmed and laughed before he put her down.

"It's like wrestling with a sow," he said. She swatted him with her gloves.

"I can't believe we're doing this," she said, taking in the spartan furnishings. Beside the bed was a large dresser and a Victorian ash and elm stick-back chair. "You can't tell anyone about this, promise."

"I promise." He made a motion of inserting an imaginary key in his mouth and turning it. He watched her face as she eyed the bed. It looked big enough to accommodate one-and-a-half people at most. "I'll sleep on the floor," he said.

She crinkled her eyes at him, and that look he'd seen before came back, only this time it had an edge of determination, like she'd made up her mind. "Let's go for a walk."

They left the hotel and headed east before climbing up the famous one hundred and ninety-nine steps to the medieval abbey at the top of the heights. Despite being ransacked by the Vikings a thousand years before, the ruins retained an inherent elegance that he thought time had yet to erode. The weight of history pressed down on him as they wandered through the adjacent cemetery where the etchings on the markers had faded over time.

"All are forgotten," he said.

"No, I don't think so." She looked around the cemetery. "Someone takes care of this place. I'm sure their memories linger on with their families and loved ones."

They headed down the slope, crossed back over the swing bridge, turning north past the colorful wooden beach huts and the few remaining beachcombers. At the edge of the waterline, they turned and looked back at the cliffs in front of them. A long, three-story, red-bricked Victorian building, framed by the fading sun, sat at the top of the bluff.

"I hear music. Do you hear it?"

"I can only hear the ocean."

"Up there," he said, pointing to the building on the cliff. "Come."

He led the way up the footpath, the music becoming louder as they drew nearer, and they soon reached the top. A sign above the double doors in the middle of the building read *Whitby Pavilion*. The words to the music were now audible. "Let Me Call You Sweetheart" mingled with the surf down below. Through the tall windows, he could see people dancing. Sebastian and Rose stood for a minute at the edge of the bluff, watching the people sway to the music. He took her by the hand, leading her up to the double doors into a large ballroom half-filled with dancers. Brown hardback chairs, the same color as the hardwood floors, lined the walls in front of the red velvet curtains. A nine-piece band was now playing "A Rainy Night in Soho" on the stage at the end of the room. He could feel the familiar pull of music taking him back to his childhood as he turned to her. "Dance?"

"Of course."

They stepped onto the dance floor, the smell of salt air wafting in through the open door, twisting and twirling the cigar and tobacco smoke like phantoms. He moved her around in a one-step.

"Very nice," Rose said, nodding her head in time to

the music. "Most of the boys I've danced with are a bit clumsy."

"We have many musicians in the family. My brother Rene plays accordion. My sister Helene sings. There is always music and dancing when the Maier family gets together. I learned to dance with my sisters and cousins. In the autumn, there is a big dance at one of the farms. All our neighbors come. That is how my parents met," he said.

"At a dance?"

"Yes, my mother lived in the next village. My father met her at the dance. She thought he would call on her, but he did not. One year after, they met again. This time, my aunt Lidia made my father call on Mother. Then they married."

"That's a sweet story," she said. "I learned to dance at school. I remember learning the waltz with Eddie Gray. I swear that boy had two left feet. I have painful memories. Literally." They circled around the floor as the band played on.

"I am glad Mr. Gray did not scare you away from dancing."

"You just have to find the right partner." Her eyes seemed to smile at him.

After another number, the band took a break. Rose and Sebastian left the pavilion and walked back to the beach, the sky cloudless and dotted with stars. The bright moon reflected on the waters of the North Sea. Sebastian pointed out the constellations to Rose.

"That is my favorite there, Lyra, the Lyre," he said pointing. "Look up. You see the three stars? Below it there are four stars, shaped like a diamond."

"How do you know all this?" she asked.

"I read an astronomy book when I was young."

She stared up at the sky. "You need a bit of

imagination to be an astronomer."

When they returned to their room that night, two glasses and a bottle of champagne sat in a bucket of chipped block ice just inside the door. A note read:

Congratulations, Newlyweds.

Arthur Greenlee

Rose popped the cork as Sebastian held out the glasses. "To Whitby," she said.

After they downed another glass with a salute to Yorkshire, she cleared her throat and studied the bed. He could tell by the distracted look in her eyes that the gears in her brain were spinning, calculating something.

"If we share the bed, will you promise to stay on your side?"

Sebastian's arms tingled. Though he was nervous, the thought of sleeping beside her intoxicated him; he couldn't say no.

"That would be proper enough. I can't have you sleeping on the floor," she said.

"Yes," he said, as his right leg started to twitch a little and he pressed his heel to the floor to hide the spasm.

They choreographed their bedtime preparations, taking turns changing into their sleepwear in the WC down the hall. Sebastian waited in his matching gray shirt and pants. Rose came into the room wearing a brown robe. They wordlessly turned back the sheets. She took off the robe, letting her dark hair spill over the white gown; it was the most beautiful sight he'd ever seen. His heart fluttered like a hummingbird. He turned off the overhead light, leaving the faint glow from the streetlamp to keep them from the dark. They lay together, shoulders rubbing, pulling the covers up to their chins, listening to the laughter and shouts of the patrons departing the pub next door. His skin turned to gooseflesh as his leg pressed against hers; he fought to keep himself from trembling.

"What are you thinking about?" she said.

"How beautiful you are when your hair is down."

"Oh, stop."

He laughed, but when it quieted for a moment, he became conscious of his chest rising and falling with each breath.

"Tell me, Mr. Astronomer, if you could be a star, which one would you be?"

"Lyra. The one I showed you earlier."

"Why?" she asked.

"I like the story. Orpheus played the lyre, he played so good, simple objects have fantastic powers. After he died, he and the lyre went to heaven as stars."

He looked up at the ceiling, relaxed a little by all the astronomy talk. Sebastian tilted his head slightly toward Rose. "Which one for you?"

"I don't know anything about the stars. I just know the North Star, and the Big Dipper. Those two aren't much to choose from." She sighed. "You know all the mythology. Which one should I be?"

Sebastian closed his eyes for a measure, grinning as he opened them again. "I know. A *sternschnuppe*, a shooting star. When people look up at the sky, and they wish for something good, they look to your star." She reached under the covers and placed her hand flat on his chest as it rose and fell. He'd never felt anything so sweet and delicate. The warnings he'd received about the pleasures of the flesh seemed ridiculous at that moment. Right here, right now, he felt more alive than he ever had before. Several seconds passed, the sound of his breathing bridged the silence between them.

"Close your eyes," she said.

"What?"

"Close your eyes."

He closed his eyes, feeling the mattress dip down as she slipped out of bed. He heard the rustle of fabric and the mattress dipped again as she slipped back into bed. Her chest pressed against him, and her breath washed against his face. *She was naked!* He froze, unsure of how to react. His hands started to shake.

"Open your eyes."

He opened his eyes; in the shadows he could make out her smile. Sebastian searched for the right words to say, but all he could come up with was, "Yes?"

"Yes," she replied.

CHAPTER TEN

England, 1914

The next morning, Sebastian got up early, quietly dressed, and went to the local newsstand. On a Sunday morning, Whitby felt like the day after a festival when all the fireworks were gone, and the town at peace. He bought the morning paper and made his way back to the room, careful not to disturb Rose. He stood in the light of the window scanning the headlines, *Serb response to ultimatum rejected. Germany says it will support Austria!* The illicit thrill of spending the night with Rose dissipated; his stomach knotted. *Not today. I'm not going to think about it today.* He sat, watching the fall and rise of the covers. She stirred in the bed for a minute before opening her eyes, sitting up, and stretching. *My God, I am the luckiest man alive.* It was more than desire. Her spirit had lit a fire in his soul, he wanted to revel in its warm embrace.

"Good morning," he said.

He chucked the newspaper into the rubbish bin and sat on the edge of the bed, taking hold of her hands.

"Sleep well?"

"I did. I dreamed we were dancing," she said.

"That was not a dream. We danced last night."

"I know that, silly. In this dream, you whispered a song in my ear while we waltzed."

"What song?"

"I couldn't make out the words. It was in French. It sounded like 'A Lady Slice of Bread,' but that can't be right." She slid out from under the covers, adjusted her gown, and stood next to him.

"Oh yes, *Il Etait une Dame Tartine*."

Sebastian stood and took Rose by the hand. They moved together in the confined space while he sang in French and then English.

One shudders seeing his Guard
made of capers and gherkins
Armed with mustard rifles
And onion peel sabres

Rose laughed, "I've never been serenaded before. I'd always imagined it would be a little more romantic than a song about food."

"It is a lullaby. My grandfather Ernst sang it to me and my brothers and sisters. His grandfather, Jacob, sang it to him when he was small."

Sebastian followed her glance to the newspaper in the rubbish bin.

"Any news?" she asked.

"They serve breakfast until ten."

"That's the headline?"

"For today," he said.

She smiled her dazzling smile, the one that always cut through him. "That's a good idea. Let's not read the paper today. Let's make the world go away."

"Bride and groom?"

"For today," she said.

He began collecting his things as she dressed. He stared at her, wanting to burnish the image into his brain.

"What?" she asked, turning around. "What are you looking at?"

"I want a picture to keep in my head."

"Oh, go on."

She turned away and stood in front of the mirror with a brush in her hand while he sat on the edge of the bed, mesmerized as her dark hair cascaded down past her shoulder blades.

"Turn around."

"Why?"

"One last look at you, before you're fully dressed. Just for two seconds."

Rose spun around, slowly counting off. "One for sorrow, two for joy." She turned away looking over her shoulder.

***

The next day, Sebastian stopped by Mr. Shaw's garage to drop off some keys before he caught his train to Hull. He was halfway out the door when Charlie stopped him.

"Hold on, I've something for you."

Charlie handed him a small photo; the one Sebastian had taken of Rose in front of the nursing school.

"I just got it developed."

Sebastian smiled. "I think she'll approve."

Charlie handed him a second photo. "I made an extra copy for you; it's the Enfield. Something to show your folks, your handiwork."

Sebastian said, "I have a secret I want to tell you before I go."

"What's that?"

"I placed an order for a ring. I am going to ask Rose to marry me."

"No, you're joking," Charlie said.

"No, true."

"Well, that's grand news; she's a fine lass," he said, shaking Sebastian's hand while clapping him on the shoulder.

"Cheers, Charlie."

"Have a safe trip, my friend."

He tucked the photos into the breast pocket of his jacket.

That evening, he stood on the fantail of the tramp steamer *Adriatic* as it passed under bridge after bridge before reaching the estuary of the River Hull. By the time it was dark, the lights of England disappeared. The ship reached Rotterdam the next day, Tuesday July 28th. The passengers were greeted with the news that Austria-Hungary had declared war on Serbia. Europe succumbed to patriotic fever, rushing to take sides. Within a week, all the major European powers were at war.

***

Rose's father dropped the bombshell that shattered her world. "I am sorry, dear. Britain and Germany are at war." He held the paper out for her to read, as if offering proof this was not some sort of extension of his dry humor. She could only read the headlines, her eyes too filled with tears to read the smaller print. But even the small print would not carry the facts that mattered to her most: Sebastian, days away from his twentieth birthday, would almost certainly be conscripted into the Kaiser's army. James moved to comfort her as if expecting her to break down, but she was numb. Her father's platitudes about the war being over quickly barely registered; the words seemed distant, meant for someone unconnected to the events that were unfolding. She needed time to think. Maybe the authorities would come to their senses and turn back this fever-train of nationalism. She left his embrace, retiring to her room to lie down. Staring up at the cracks in the ceiling, she wanted to sleep, hoping to dream Sebastian back into her life.

The dreams came the next night. Rose finds herself walking the rolling hills of a countryside dotted with farms and tidy houses, the sound of church bells chiming from the nearby village. The surroundings feel familiar, but she can't place the location. Black clouds roll in from the eastern horizon as she passes through the gate of the village cemetery. Inside, confronted by row after row of tombs marked with German names and a death date of 1914, she is seized by fear that Sebastian is one of them. She rushes from one marker to the next, searching for his name, but does not find it. Drained, a sense of relief settles in until she notices a single tomb further up the slope of the hill. In front of it, a man wearing clothes cut of an unusual fashion, stands silhouetted against the overcast sky. From behind, it looks like Sebastian. Could it be? Her heart thumps against her breastbone as she rushes to him, touching his elbow, "Sebastian."

Her spirit sinks, it's not him. He is of a similar stature, but his eyes are liquid-brown instead of striking-blue. Sebastian's amulet is visible above his open-collared shirt; this only unsettles her more. She recognizes the distinctive oval shape of the individual links. *I bought that chain for him, but never had the chance to give it to him.* She wanted to ask him how he came into possession of it, but he speaks first, his voice like an echo as he fingers the amulet. "Now the story can be told," he says in an American accent. He points to the grave. A sense of foreboding grips her heart; her blood runs cold as she follows his gaze to the marker.

The inscription reads: *Sebastian Maier.* A gasp escapes her lips. Stomach churning, she rushes to the slab and runs her fingers along the etchings as if they will offer an answer. Angry at herself for being afraid, she fights back her fear, lashing out at the man. "What does this mean?" she demands, turning to face him. "Who are you?" The sound of her voice wakes her from the dream.

CHAPTER ELEVEN

France, 1916

Rose woke early and splashed her face and underarms with water from the basin on her night table. She brushed her teeth, put her hair up, and dressed for the day: a faded blue dress, a white apron with a Red Cross emblem, and white oversleeves. Her skirt, shortened to avoid the mud, revealed a pair of gum boots her parents had mailed her at Christmas. She packed her sleeping kit and some underclothes into a small valise and headed out to the courtyard of the converted chateau where her ride was waiting. Rose and a Scottish nurse named Eliza were being temporarily transferred, from the chateau that served as a hospital, to a casualty clearing station in anticipation of the British summer offensive on the River Somme.

The driver put their bags in the back of the lorry and helped them up. The canvas cover had been rolled back, exposing the ribs on the side, allowing the summer breeze to pass through. Just as they were about to depart, three young soldiers approached the driver, speaking with him briefly before he pointed to the back of the truck. The trio came around, slinging their kit bags and rifles into the back. The young men nudged and winked at one another at the sight of the nurses as they clambered aboard. They looked like teenagers to Rose, reminding her of boys she knew in school. The youngest looking, a handsome lad with blond hair, and a gap-tooth smile said, "Hullo ladies, come here often?"

The two women chuckled, shaking their heads.

"I'm Johnny. These are my mates, Gilly and Robbo."

"I'm Rose."

"Eliza."

The blond soldier pressed on, "We're with the 11th battalion, we're trying to catch up with our regiment, the East Lancashires."

Their uniforms, although slightly mismatched, were in excellent condition. The boys looked freshly scrubbed. She thought they should be studying for exams instead of heading to the front. "How old are you?"

Johnny said, "Nineteen." The others grinned and nodded. "We're pals, schoolmates from Accrington. Granby secondary school. We signed up together; didn't want to miss out on the show."

Rose winced, *You've no idea.*

"Have you been here long?" he asked.

"Eleven months," she said.

"Seven months," said Eliza.

"We just arrived; we want to get stuck in," he said. "Wrap things up so we can be home by Christmas."

"Let's hope so," Rose replied.

"I'll come see you when it's over. We'll have a drink to celebrate."

She couldn't remember being that innocent. "That sounds nice."

The lorry trundled down the bumpy road, passing

columns of khaki-clad soldiers and horse-drawn carts carrying metal ammunition boxes. Further along, huge ugly scars in the earth and mounds of shell casings piled up next to the ravaged poplars lining the country lane. The rumble of cannons grew louder as they neared the front. Rose saw the smiles on the three soldiers' faces disappear when they arrived at a small village that had been shelled earlier. Through the shattered wall of one of the houses, splintered timbers sprawled at oblique angles, the salon scored black, decorated by a brass bed on top of an upright piano. The driver stopped the truck, shouting to the men that this was where they got off. The boys gathered their bags and rifles and climbed down. Johnny turned to Rose before he left. "Don't forget, we'll have a drink."

"I won't forget. Good luck, Johnny."

Ten minutes later, the truck passed an apple orchard next to a cemetery filled with simple wooden crosses. The driver dropped them at a two-story, century-old convent with a mustard-colored tile roof partially covered by camouflage netting. The clearing station was across the rutted road in a converted school where the sisters used to teach. Inside the convent, the head nurse, Edith, directed them to their billets on the upper floor. The windows of their shared room looked out on a little green garden with a tulip tree in the center. The room was furnished with two beds and a well-worn armoire. It wasn't as nice as her quarters at the hospital, but Rose wasn't disappointed; she had not expected anything nice this close to the front.

In the evening, they sat out on the sill, watching the outgoing artillery arc across the black sky like yellow rainbows, the windowpane shimmied a little with each explosion, and the faint smell of cordite wafted into their room. Rose slowly caressed the crucifix around her neck, watching the rockets' glare before she got up from the sill. She retrieved a small flask from her valise, unscrewed the cap, and took a swig before handing it to Eliza. "Brandy."

***

The next morning, Rose opened her eyes to see her roommate staring out into the courtyard as if straining to hear something. She tried to read the expression on her colleague's face as Eliza turned from the window and said, "Listen."

She removed the cotton stuffed into her ears and raised herself on her elbows, cocking her head to the window. Birds chirping mingled with the murmur of voices from the garden below. "I don't hear anything."

"The artillery stopped," Eliza replied.

Rose slumped back on her pillow, closed her eyes, and put her hands over her face. "Time for the infantry to go in, time to go to work." She threw the covers back and rolled out of bed. "Here we go again."

Eliza answered, "Same old song again," pressing her lips to her crucifix.

Two hours later, ambulances began arriving. Rose and the other nurses scrambled to unload the British soldiers. The men's faces were sunburnt, uniforms caked in dirt, field dressings the color of burgundy. Some were labeled with bright red stripes, indicating they might hemorrhage at any moment; others were missing limbs. The wounded came in wave after wave, flooding the clearing station, overwhelming the doctors and nurses. When they ran out of beds, some of the men were placed on the floor, in corridors, in the gymnasium, and even the dining hall. The humid air hung heavy with the odor of mud, blood, sweat, urine, and feces.

Rose poured herself into the work. With quiet efficiency, she cut clothes off soldiers, washed away the grime, and dressed their wounds. This process was repeated as bloodstained clothes, soiled bandages, and soldiers' gear piled up around the room. The persistent moaning and cries for help plucked her nerves. By fixing her attention on the sound of a soldier tunelessly singing "Abide with Me," she found herself carried back to her childhood. Sunday mornings and church with her father. For a moment, the thought of a better time raised her spirits, but only for a moment.

As evening came on, the pace slowed a little. Rose checked on one of the new arrivals. The young soldier's blond hair was matted, and wet, crusty crimson specks formed around his mouth. She wiped the blood away and a shock of recognition hit her. It was Johnny, the boy she had met on the ride over. Her attention was drawn to the large bandage on his left side. She leaned down and gently pulled the white strip back, revealing a gaping wound. A shell had sliced him open from armpit to hip, and his internal organs threatened to slip out. *He won't survive the night.*

The young man's eyes fluttered open. In a voice barely above a whisper he asked, "Where am I?"

"You're in the hospital."

He squinted at Rose as if trying to focus.

"You're the nurse from the other day."

"Yes, that's right."

"Am I going to be alright?"

She took hold of his hand and said, "Yes, the doctor's going to fix you up. You'll be dancing with your girl in no time."

"I haven't got a girl."

A fit of despair settled in her gut. She wondered how this fit in with God's master plan. "Get well, Johnny.

When you get back home, the girls will be fighting over you."

Rose let go of his hand and went to check on another patient. When she returned thirty minutes later, Johnny was dead. Her heart sank at the thought of how his parents back in Lancashire would receive the news. But she shed no tears of sorrow. She simply closed his eyes and moved to the next patient.

Morning broke, sunshine bled through the clouds, bathing the staff and the incoming soldiers in a soft light. Rain returned after noon and lasted until early evening. Then it was night once more. The next day was no better. The wounded poured in and the doctors and nurses silently cursed the sound of the approaching ambulances. Rose's feet hurt, her back ached, her short-term memory failed, and she began to second guess her every decision.

As darkness deepened on the third day, they brought in a wounded German soldier and put him in a bed across from where Rose was tending to a Welsh fusilier. She'd seen wounded enemy soldiers before. In the beginning, she'd held out hope that Sebastian would be among them, not wounded too badly, just enough to be brought here where she could see him. But they were usually too blond, too fat, or too short to be Sebastian.

After seeing so many bodies with arms and legs blown off, she prayed not to see him again, not torn up and twisted like all the others. But this one looked like him: the long limbs, the lean torso, and the same shock of dark hair spilling out from underneath the bandage covering his eyes. *You're tired; your mind's playing tricks on you,* she rationalized. After changing the dressing on the legless corporal, she stepped in front of the German, staring at him, trying to remember the details of Sebastian's body from that night at the beach.

Edith, busy checking his bandages, turned to Rose, "Is everything all right?"

"Who is he?"

"I don't remember; it's on the chart there in front of you if you need to know. Doesn't matter, he'll be lucky if he's alive in the morning."

Rose stared at the chart, but her vision blurred. "Can you read the name for me? My eyes are tired."

Edith shot her a quizzical look and moved next to Rose. "Sure." She pulled the chart up, flipped back the first page, eyes scanning the text. Rose sucked in a breath of air and held it. "Grabowski, Albert." The tension escaped from her body as she exhaled, her knees buckled, and she reeled under the weight of forty-eight hours with no sleep. She fell into Edith's arms. The head nurse guided her outside, the cool evening air momentarily reviving her. "Go, get a few hours rest. This shows no sign of letting up," Edith told her.

Rose staggered out of the clearing station, stumbling the short distance to the convent. Pumped up with adrenaline, unable to sleep, she sat staring out the window at the tangled moonlit shadows cast by the apple trees on the rows of freshly dug graves in the cemetery. The relief that had flooded through her body with the knowledge that the young soldier was not Sebastian slowly ebbed away. Life near the front was a zero-sum gain. She realized her sense of relief meant that back in Berlin, or Munich, a German mother would never see her son again. If Sebastian was alive, he would be out there getting showered with shells and bullets, awaiting the next roll of the dice. She felt as empty as the flask in her trembling hand.

CHAPTER TWELVE

France, 1916

"Help me!" a voice shouted in English. Sebastian and the new ambulance driver, Gerd, navigated their way through the maze of zig-zagged trenches with their stretcher full of field dressings and Red Cross care packages. Beads of sweat formed on the faces of the two ambulancemen as they bore through the earth, passing squads of haggard-looking infantrymen playing Skat and smoking cigarettes. They arrived at the supply line, dropping their load at the underground dugout occupied by the medics. Sebastian heard a voice cry out again, "Help me!"

Closer to the front, the groans and moans were impossible to ignore. "I need help!"

He asked Gerd, "Did you hear that?"

"How could I not?"

The pair followed the supply line trench for another forty meters before turning right onto the communications line. Rats scurried away at their approach, a passing soldier speared one with his bayonet, flinging it up and over the parapet. The smells of the trenches—decaying flesh, overflowing latrines, and disinfectant—grew stronger as they approached the main line another fifty meters on.

A mustachioed sergeant standing nearby in a tattered uniform lit his pipe.

"Where's that shouting coming from?" Sebastian asked.

The sergeant pointed his thumb over his shoulder toward the British trenches. "Out there. He's in a bomb crater," he said with a heavy Stuttgart accent. "We can't see him, but by the sound of it, he's about thirty meters away."

Sebastian spied a trench periscope next to the scaling ladder. He adjusted the viewfinder and saw barbed wire and blasted-out patches of earth. In the background, sandbags marked the British lines, no sign of the wounded man. It was too risky for the Tommies to try to retrieve him; they would lose two or three men to save one.

"Help me! For the love of God, help me," the voice pleaded.

"He's been whining ever since we sent the morning artillery over to the other side," the sergeant said.

Sebastian looked at Gerd, who shrugged. Sebastian had cheated death countless times before. He took a perverse pleasure in knowing there was no rhyme or reason why one man survived, and another did not. The new men, the replacements, told him he was lucky, but he knew otherwise. It was just a game of chance. Now, it was as if the spirits of the dead were urging him on, challenging him to risk it all again. He walked over to the edge of the parapet and shouted in English, "Hello, Tommy in the trenches, can you hear me?" No response. "Tommy, can you hear me?"

A voice shouted back from the other side, "We hear you Fritz, what do you want?"

"There is a wounded British soldier in front of our position," Sebastian said.

"We know."

"We will bring him in. Will you promise not to shoot?"

A long pause ensued. Sebastian imagined they must be conferring. A voice called out, "Okay, Fritz. Send two men to get him. No funny business!"

He turned to the Sergeant, "The British have agreed to let us retrieve the wounded man. Can you tell your men to hold their fire?"

The sergeant raised his eyebrows, "Sure." He turned to pass the message down the line.

Sebastian heard the British soldiers shouting, "Hold your fire!"

He paused to let the word spread to the German troops before he shouted back across No Man's Land, "We are coming!"

"All right, get on with it," came the response.

He looked at Gerd and said, "Let's go."

"Me?" he said with a tone of incredulity.

"Who else? I can't do it alone."

"It's a Tommy; it's not our concern."

"He's a Christian, just like you." Gerd looked away. "Are you afraid you're going to get shot?" Sebastian motioned to the east. "The generals are going to kill us all eventually. Might as well get it over with."

Gerd shook his head. His shoulders slumped. "Ah, shit!"

"That's the spirit. We shall walk through the Valley of the Shadow of Death, and we shall fear no evil. We've red crosses on our sleeves." The sergeant laughed and relit his pipe.

Heart racing, Sebastian slowly climbed up the ladder step-by-step and went over the top. Standing erect, hands spread wide, he braced for the impact, senses on high alert, ears attuned to every little sound, waiting for the bullet with his name on it. Seconds ticked by; one for sorrow, two for joy… Gerd handed the stretcher up and climbed and stood next to him.

"You're going to get us fucking killed," he hissed.

The terrain, a pockmarked mess of large and small bomb craters was littered with dead soldiers, shell casings, and smashed equipment, the sickly-sweet smell far worse than in the trenches. Sebastian called out to the man.

"Hello, we are coming. Where are you?"

"Over 'ere."

The voice came from twenty meters to the right of their position. Like circus artists walking a tightrope, they carefully threaded their way through a small gap in the barbed wire and reached a bomb crater six meters long by five meters wide. The wounded man lay at the bottom with two dead soldiers face down in the mud below his feet. In their filthy uniforms, it was difficult to tell if they were British or German. The two men quickly clambered down to the injured soldier. He smiled weakly at them as they knelt beside him but could not hide the look of desperation in his eyes. Sebastian did a quick inspection of the man: uniform torn at the edges, no helmet. He pulled back the crimson-colored trousers from the soldier's hip to check the wound, making a quick diagnosis: he's lost some blood, and he'll probably walk with a limp, but he should make it. He asked the man, "What is your name?"

"Wright, William, Private."

"We are taking you to a German hospital. Wiener schnitzel and blonde *frauleins*. For you, the war is kaput."

Sebastian told Gerd, "Let's move him on to the stretcher." He turned to William, switching back to English, "William, we will lift you now, it will hurt."

"I don't care, just get me out of 'ere."

Sebastian looked at Gerd. *"Eins, zwei, drei."*

They lifted the wounded man, who let out a yelp as they placed him on the blood-stained stretcher. They hoisted him up and out of the crater. Sebastian focused on carrying the man back as gently as possible, but he couldn't block out the voice in his head reminding him that he was utterly exposed now. His thumping heart sounded out a drumbeat rhythm, an invitation to dance with death, a requiem for his soul. Safety, only twenty-five meters east, seemed like another country. They picked their way through the maze of barbed wire, rats scampered out of their way. William grimaced and grunted but said nothing. They reached the parapet and handed the fallen warrior to the infantrymen, who gently lowered him to the wooden boardwalk at the bottom of the trench. Gerd scrambled to the safety of the trench and Sebastian followed.

Gerd's body shook as he slid down the wall of the trench and sat on the shooting perch. "Jesus, don't do that to me again." He fumbled for a cigarette, which he tried to light, but his hands shook violently, the match burned his fingers before he dropped it between the slats below his feet. The sergeant struck a match and lit his cigarette for him. Gerd nodded thanks as he sucked in the smoke.

William had a relieved look on his face. He reached up and took hold of Sebastian's hand, "Thank you."

For a moment, hope filled Sebastian's heart, providing a glimpse into something beyond the despair that normally enveloped him. It was an alien sensation. He'd become so accustomed to living without hope as a means of staying sane, living with it seemed an act of madness.

CHAPTER THIRTEEN

France, 1916

A few days after the rescue mission, Sebastian was summoned to see his commanding officer. Fearing that he might be in trouble for risking his life for a British soldier, he straightened his gray tunic, removed his field cap, and combed his hair before entering the captain's quarters. Herr Witzel sat behind a desk, smoking a cigarette from a holder as Sebastian saluted.

"Reporting as ordered, Sir." His palms felt slick with sweat.

Witzel leaned his head back slightly and blew out a lungful of smoke. "I hear you speak English. Is that true?"

"Yes, sir." Sebastian's shoulders tensed, bracing for a tongue-lashing over his impulsive act.

"Good, I have an assignment for you. Our medical director has been in contact with his counterpart in the British army. We have arranged for an exchange of eight seriously wounded prisoners. They are being brought over from Lazarett Saint-Clement today. You will be traveling behind enemy lines to the town of Revigny sur Ornain, where the British hospital is located. You and

Krummenacher will be the drivers; a German-speaking British officer and his aide will accompany you. Any questions?"

Relieved he was not to be disciplined, the tension slipped away, and he breathed easier. "When do we leave sir?"

"Tomorrow, 8 am. Report back here."

***

That night, Sebastian lay in the back of the ambulance, looking up at the battered roof. He pulled out his photograph of Rose. *How are you getting on?* he wondered. An idea came to him! Maybe he could get one of the English soldiers to mail a letter to her. Suddenly inspired, he sat up and rummaged through his pack, pulling out his gloves, knit cap, and scarf—winter gear that had been shoved to the bottom months ago. Underneath was a small, black German-English phrase book that he had brought back from England.

When the war had started two years ago, there had been a sense of optimism: A decisive victory and the men would be home by Christmas. Seduced by this thinking, his dreams were filled with happy fantasies of reuniting with his sweetheart. He wrote to Rose, telling her how beautiful she looked that Sunday morning in Whitby standing in front of the tilt mirror. The image of her with a comb in her hand, dark hair spilling over her shoulders and down her camisole, warmed his bones in the chill air. He saved the letters for the day when peace would be restored, and he could mail them out. By the time the first anniversary of the war passed, three drivers in his ambulance company had been killed by chlorine gas, and he no longer believed it was his destiny to make it out alive. He threw the letters away.

He read the words underlined in the book so long ago: *Always, heart, someday,* thinking how innocent he had been. He wondered if Rose would recognize the man he'd become—bitter, cynical, no longer in love with life. Setting his pencil to paper, he began composing a letter, flipping back and forth through the little black English-German dictionary. He blocked out all the unwanted traits he'd acquired, searching for a little light in the darkness of his soul, giving voice to the man he'd once been. He crumpled the first draft, wrote a second, and threw that away as well. He read the third draft twice, folded it, and stuffed it into an envelope.

***

The next day, Sebastian sat at the wheel of his ambulance truck, following a dirt road over the countryside. Hans Krummenacher trailed behind; small white flags tied to each of their vehicles. The crossing point was a small village that had been on the front line since the war's early days, changing hands numerous times. A German infantry captain waved them through. The town was nothing more than shattered buildings and bits and pieces of scattered rubble. He wondered what had happened to the inhabitants and if they would come back.

They slowed to a crawl, slipping past barbed wire and barricades that had been pulled back. On the other side, a British officer and an enlisted man stood next to a dust-covered Enfield motorcycle. The officer introduced himself as Harris and instructed Sebastian and Hans to follow him. Once past the village, the road smoothed out. The foul smell of the front dissipated; the aroma of clover filled the air. The barbed wire and trenches became fields of wheat and farmhouse gardens with radishes and tomatoes. The clean air, scrubbed of the smells of decay, reminded him of home.

Further along, a train of horse-drawn carts headed back to the front. The fact that they were carrying supplies for the next attack was not lost on Sebastian. He marveled at how pastoral everything was so close to the front, imagining the quiet country sounds of sheep bleating and dogs barking, followed by the distant thunder of a major offensive. They passed an artillery company where the soldiers washed their clothes beside several racks of shells. The cannoneers looked at the two German soldiers with great curiosity.

The convoy continued down the dusty road, a flour-like coating obscuring the markings on their vehicles. They turned off the main road and soon arrived at the converted chateau that served as a hospital. With the help of the British staff, they offloaded the wounded men. Before they took on the German wounded, one of the staffers appeared with two small towels and a small white basin half-filled with water.

"Would you care to wash up and have some tea and biscuits with us?"

Surprised by this act of hospitality, it took his brain a few seconds to think in English. "Yes, thank you."

Sebastian and Hans took turns scrubbing the layer of grime off their faces and hands. When they were done, they joined the hospital personnel in the courtyard, standing around a small table, eating biscuits, and drinking tea. Beyond "please," "thank you," and "you're welcome," there was little conversation until Sebastian turned to the motorbike driver. "How do you like the bike?"

The driver paused before answering. "I like her just fine," he said guardedly.

"I worked in a motorbike shop in England,"

Sebastian said.

"Oh, aye," said the driver, seeming to warm to the conversation. "Maybe you can help. Sometimes the engine revs up when you shift into high gear. I have to slow down, downshift, and shift up again, sometimes two or three times. It's a real pain."

Sebastian told him, "These motors will do that in warm weather. Next time pull back on the throttle, and then up slowly."

A nurse walked by, stopped, and stared wide-eyed, as if seeing a ghost.

CHAPTER FOURTEEN

France, 1916

The morning sun climbed the walls of Chateau Faux Miroir, poking through the broken shutters on the window of Rose's tiny room. Streaks of light hit her face, forcing her to wake up. The air had cooled a bit overnight, allowing her to doze off earlier than usual, leaving her feeling rested for the first time in a long while. After her difficult spell at the clearing station, she was glad to be back in the relative comfort of the chateau. She opened the shutters looking out onto the courtyard and was greeted by the familiar sight of a Royal Enfield motorcycle parked in the gravel lot adjacent to the chateau. A ruddy-faced man in an enlisted uniform stood next to it smoking a cigarette. Rose left her room, went downstairs, and approached the soldier.

"Nice bike," she said.

The man smiled, answering with a Scottish accent, "Oh, yes, ma'am. She's a beauty."

"I had a gentleman friend back in England with a bike like this. We used to ride up and down the Dales. It was a lot of fun."

His eyes met hers, but she didn't look away. "Well, maybe when I get back, I'll take you for a ride."

"Maybe," she replied, going off to make her rounds.

Today, they would be exchanging wounded prisoners. Rose went through each German's paperwork to make sure all was in order. A little before noon came the unmistakable whine of the Royal Enfield. Through the window she saw a bike and two German ambulances coming over the dusty rise. She exited the building, emerging into the midday sun, having made up her mind to take the Scotsman up on his offer. She was tired of being lonely and needed a distraction from the grimness of a wartime hospital.

Rose strolled over to where several of the staff members and the German drivers were standing and drinking tea. The gray uniforms of the German drivers stood in sharp contrast to the khaki-colored British ones. The Scotsman tried to catch her gaze, but her attention was drawn to the taller German soldier. *Impossible!*

It was Sebastian.

She'd read somewhere about people describing the moment before they were hit by lightning and thought it must have felt like this. Her heart seemed to pause a measure, her arms tingled, and some unseen force of nature embraced her, pulling her forward. "Sebastian?" she said, afraid to break the spell, afraid her mind was playing tricks on her.

The young man turned to her with a look of surprise. "Yes."

Her pulse raced ahead of her thoughts, and she paused to let the words catch up.

"It's me, Rose."

It took a moment for him to speak. His lips moved, but only a small gasp escaped from his throat. His face creased in a huge smile, and he shouted, "Rose! *Mein*

Gott in Himmel!" He rushed to wrap his arms around her, nearly knocking her off her feet. She felt unbalanced, unprepared for the reunion she had once fantasized about. It wasn't supposed to be like this. It had taken a long time for her to accept that they were never to be together again. His being here filled her with guilt for giving up hope, for thinking he was dead. Their embrace produced sharp looks from the other hospital staff, and she self-consciously stepped back from Sebastian, pushing him gently away. Confusion shone in his face, the smile falling away, before the light of reason returned to his eyes.

"I know this woman," he said, holding the palms of his hands up as if to show no ill intent. "We … we knew each other in England." The hospital staff all nodded their heads as one, eyeing them with great interest. Sebastian and Rose stepped out of earshot of the group. She could feel a dozen heads swiveling and tracking their movements.

"You look fantastic," Sebastian blurted.

The lines on his face were foreign to her, but his eyes were as clear and as bright as ever. She took in a deep breath, composing herself, afraid to say the wrong thing. She wanted to tell him how the very thought of him brought light during her darkest hours, giving strength when most needed. "You look a little dusty." She kicked herself for offering such a mundane observation, but he laughed, trying to brush the dust off his tunic.

"It was a long drive."

"How are you?" she asked.

"Good," he replied. "And you?"

"I'm holding up."

He looked closely at her, and she saw herself in his eyes, suddenly aware of how much she'd changed in the last two years. What must he think of me? I'm not the same girl he knew. It's obvious even to a blind man. She looked away, shoving her hands into her pockets, unsure of what to do next. A pregnant pause filled the air. "I have something for you. Do you still have your amulet?"

Sebastian pulled the amulet out of his tunic pocket. "Of course," he said, holding it up. "My good luck charm."

Rose undid the chain from around her neck, removed the crucifix she was wearing, and put it in her pocket. She took Sebastian's amulet, affixed the chain clasp around the hook. She wanted to place it around his neck just to feel the touch of his flesh against hers but thought she had pushed her luck far enough already and placed it in his hand instead. A spark of electricity seemed to pass between them for a moment. "I always thought that amulet needed a chain. I bought this for your birthday."

He placed it around his neck, running his fingers along the chain and amulet. "Thank you." Sebastian stared at his feet, appearing to weigh something in his mind. She braced herself for awful news, her mental reflexes conditioned to look for the dark clouds that accompanied a silver lining. He looked up, a smile flickering across his face. "At one time, I felt guilty about lying to the owner of the Hotel in Whitby. We told him we were going to Scotland for our honeymoon, remember? The champagne?"

"I remember that it was cheap champagne."

"Yes, but we did not say the truth."

"We told a little lie. It doesn't matter now," she said, shrugging her shoulders. "You used to feel guilty … not anymore?"

He looked down for a second before meeting her eyes again. "Standing here now, I have no regrets. When I feel bad, I remember those times, and it reminds me that there is a reason to live."

Her heart swelled with a desire for him to hold her, tell her everything would be all right, just like it used to be. One of the doctors coughed loudly in almost theatrical fashion as if urging her to wrap things up. She stepped forward to kiss him on the cheek, but out of the corner of her eye, Rose could see the disapproving look on the face of her commanding officer. She stopped in mid-step and put her hand on Sebastian's forearm. "I must go. Take care of yourself."

"You as well."

She turned to leave. "Wait. I have something for you," he said, as he pulled out an envelope. "I wrote this last night, and I was going to … ask one of the British drivers to post it. It is probably forbidden. A letter for you."

"Thank you." She hesitated, wondering how this small act of kindness would be interpreted by her superiors. But her desire to read this letter overcame her anxiety. *Fallout be damned*, she thought. What are they going to do? Send me to the war? The contents of that letter meant more than anything else in the world. She took the letter and secreted it in her pocket. "Thank you." This time, he turned to go first.

"Sebastian," she called out. He paused mid-step, pivoting back to her. "I've no regrets either; it was the best of times."

He smiled in return, but the sadness in his face was as plain as words on a page. Rose hurried to the hospital, a jumble of thoughts racing through her head. The mental callouses she had formed over the last year slowly peeled away; raw emotions threatened to run free. Heartbroken, that was the word that her friend Cora used to describe her separation from Sebastian. "You must be heartbroken, dear." Heartbroken, as if you could hold the broken pieces of your dreams in your hands. She'd learned from her time in France that hearts were soft things that bruise easily. The pain lingered like an invisible scar that you only need run your fingers over to revive. Seeing herself in his eyes struck a raw nerve, her hands trembled, and she made a fist to stop the shaking. Once inside the hospital, Rose distracted herself with sterilizing instruments until she heard engines sputtering to life. She walked back to the front entrance, standing on the steps as the ambulances and the Enfield started back to the front. Out of habit, she reached for the spot where the crucifix had been.

***

Later that evening, Rose lay on her bunk, staring up at the fan slowly spinning overhead as her equilibrium returned. Her relationship with Sebastian had a perfectness about it. They'd be forever young, roaming the quiet country lanes on that motorcycle. Maybe it was the naïveté of that notion that bothered her so much or maybe it was him seeing her as she was now, broken and put back together. Outside, the sun slowly faded into a red orange glow. She pulled Sebastian's letter out, slicing it open with a nail file, straining to make out the words in the dim light.

Rose,
I hope you are well. I never got a chance to properly say goodbye. I want you to know that I am fine. I have a safe job as an ambulance driver. My skill as a mechanic served me well. I also have my amulet and your photo for good luck.
We were together only a short time, but something happened to us. Our hearts were full of hope. I was so

happy, all I needed was you. I cherish the memories of the two of us riding that Enfield around Yorkshire. I wish you the best.
    With love,
    Sebastian

Rose shivered, a slow parade of tears streamed down her cheeks, her hands trembled. A primal sense of lonesomeness shrouded her in a fog of despair. Just twenty-one, she felt old, used up. *Jesus, stop feeling sorry for yourself.* She blew her nose, rubbed her eyes, and picked up her King James Bible from the nightstand, placing the letter inside the Book of Luke. Putting the book next to the basin, she lay back down. Deflated and unable to sleep, she rolled from her bunk, went to her nightstand, and splashed water on her face. Stepping outside into the cool evening air, a light breeze deliciously chilled her damp skin. Looking straight up into the clear sky, it was easy to find Vega. Next to the waning crescent moon she could make out Lyra, shining right in front of her. Right where it had been the whole time.

CHAPTER FIFTEEN

Germany, 1918

By August, the German lines had been pushed back toward the town of Metz. Sebastian's ambulance company was bivouacked near the village of Pont-a-Mousson. It was there he met Yvette Gehrig. Tall, with pale skin and hazel eyes, she retained an inner calm despite the dire circumstances of a wartime hospital. Sebastian told her she reminded him of an old Alsatian folk song and was secretly thrilled when she blushed as he recited the words about a maiden with "raven black hair having a luster like moonlight shining on a lonely hill." Sebastian, Gerd, and Hans would drink tea and chat with the nurses, regaling them with amusing stories of their trips to the front and sharing tidbits of embarrassing information about each other. He sought her out at the hospital, and they would take a moment to sit and talk about their hometowns in Alsace. Something about her reminded him of Rose. That same kind of light seemed to glow within her, he found it alluring. It took him by surprise, for the first time in a long time, he didn't fall into a deep melancholy at the thought of his lost love.

On the morning of the last day of September, the three remaining ambulances trundled down the rutted road, heading west to collect the latest casualties from the big push by the Allies. Sebastian was on point, followed by Gerd, with Hans bringing up the rear. They reached the staging area just behind the lines, working quickly and efficiently to load the wounded as artillery shells exploded a few kilometers away. On the return leg, Sebastian had just rounded a splintered oak tree when he heard a klaxon sound. He leaned out, craning his neck, and saw Hans' truck pulled over to the side with steam coming out of the engine. Gerd stopped alongside Sebastian, and they ran back to the ailing vehicle. The three of them removed the engine cover and Sebastian immediately spied a hose missing a clamp.

"I've got a spare clamp in my truck, let me get it. Gerd, you go on ahead and we'll catch up."

Gerd nodded and ran to his ambulance. He shouted over his shoulder before he climbed in, "Last one back buys the first round!" Then he roared away down the road that stretched out over the countryside to the east.

Sebastian ran back to his truck, gathered the tools he needed, and fixed the broken hose in a few minutes. He looked at Hans and grinned. "Gerd's a slow driver; we can beat him. I know a shortcut."

They jumped in their vehicles and motored down the country lane, splashing through the occasional puddle, careful not to jolt their passengers. The roads, softened by the rains but not yet sloppy, were in fair condition. Sebastian knew if they got in sight of Gerd before he got out of the old peach orchard, they could pass him in the meadow where the lane widened. As Sebastian gunned the motor, he caught sight of Gerd just as he was emerging into the open fields. Sixty seconds later, he drew up alongside and laid on the klaxon. Gerd flinched and his truck swerved to the right as Sebastian shot past. Seconds later, he heard the klaxon and guessed that Hans had passed Gerd as well. He leaned out, looking back at Hans giving him the thumbs up. Beyond him, he could see Gerd yelling something but couldn't make out what he was saying. Over the roar of the engine, he thought he heard a high-pitched whistling sound. His muscles tensed. *Artillery.* They had no cover, nowhere to hide. When he looked over his shoulder again, Gerd's ambulance exploded in a brilliant flash of orange and yellow light. The blast rattled Sebastian's truck. Automobile and body parts rained down on the scarred green meadow. He slammed on the brakes. Hans skidded to a halt behind him. They leapt from their vehicles and ran back, gaping at the flames licking the skeletal remains of their friend's ambulance.

When the whine of artillery made an encore appearance, they instinctively sprinted for their vehicles. Adrenaline surged through Sebastian's body as a shell burst two hundred meters to their left. Hans got to his truck first and roared past. Sebastian jumped in the cab of his vehicle, jamming it into gear. His heart pounded like a bass drum as another shell exploded one hundred meters to the right. He mashed the accelerator to the floor, the truck bolted forward, lurching down the road. The wounded men in the back screamed for him to slow down. He ignored their shouts, straining to listen for the next round. The fourth shell blew up two hundred meters behind them. By the time the fifth shell dropped, he and Hans were half a kilometer away. He breathed a momentary sigh of relief before remembering what had happened to his friend.

Yvette was there to receive him as he followed Hans into the hospital grounds. The worried look in her hazel eyes dissipated when they met his, and he saw her shoulders relax a little. He busied himself with the offloading of the wounded, wanting to avoid having to tell Yvette or any of the other hospital staff the bad news right away. He'd wait until he had a drink first.

***

Later that evening, when things slowed, Sebastian sat on a bench in the small courtyard, framed by head-high arborvitae that looked black, barely distinguishable from the night sky. He drank from a flask, eating a biscuit as he scanned the patchy clouds. A nurse exited the building. Even in the dark he could tell by the way she walked that it was Yvette. He shifted to make room for her to sit next to him. He swallowed the last of his biscuit, washing it down with a slug from the flask. He looked at his feet and scuffed some mud off the soles of his boots. She placed a hand on his shoulder. "I'm so sorry about Gerd."

Sebastian, worn down, defeated, lifted his gaze. "Hans is writing a letter to Gerd's parents. Their families knew each other back in Wurzburg." Tears welled up in his eyes, "It should've been me. If I hadn't stopped to help Hans, I would have been right where Gerd was. If I had told him to wait, he'd be here, and I'd be out there." He croaked out the words, "I think I got him killed." He sobbed for a few seconds before rubbing his eyes with the backs of his hands. "I'm sorry, I can't do this anymore. The lives we're living, the things we say and do, they're like words in a book that will never be read. Nobody will ever understand the things we've seen."

His heart ached. She took his hand in hers, squeezing it gently. "It does no good to think like that."

He took several deep breaths before shaking his head and saying unconvincingly, "You're right." He squared his shoulders, attempting to shrug off the melancholy. "Let's talk about something else. Tell me, how did you end up here?"

"I volunteered."

"Why, feeling patriotic?"

"No. My brother, Paul, was killed at Verdun. I felt I had to do something. My parents were against it; they didn't want to lose another child. But I did it anyway. Later, my father told me he was proud of me."

"Sorry about your brother."

"It was hard on my father; Paul wanted to be a carpenter just like him. He would sing while Papa played the violin; they were like two peas in the same pod." An easy smile played across her face, but the hint of longing revealed the emptiness in her soul. "When we heard the news, it was like I was living in a house of pain, a prison. I couldn't bear to see the sadness in my father's face. That was part of my reason for leaving as well. I couldn't take it anymore. I had to get out."

Some other staff members came out into the courtyard, and Yvette released her gentle grip. Cigarettes were passed around, and Sebastian shared the contents of his flask. After everyone drank a toast to Gerd, they speculated on how soon the war would end and what they would do after returning home. The brief reverie ended when they heard the rumble of artillery in the distance and saw the faint outline of yellow flashes against the night sky. Everyone knew it was only a matter of time before more casualties arrived. The glowing red lights of their cigarettes were snuffed out one by one, and a few people made the sign of the cross. The caregivers left the peaceful respite of the courtyard to get back to work. Sebastian and Yvette were the last to go. He reached for her hand as the two of them trailed behind the others and she slowly interlaced her fingers with his.

From inside, he could hear orders being shouted over the clatter of drawers opening and closing. They stopped in front of the door, and he turned to face her. Yvette placed her hand on Sebastian's unbuttoned tunic and stared at the amulet he wore around his neck. When she looked up to meet his gaze, he stroked the side of her face with the back of his hand, leaned in close, and gave her a long, lingering kiss. The softness of her lips intoxicated him; this small moment of connection lifted him out of despair. When they stopped kissing, he held her for several long seconds. Time slowed; an overwhelming desire to stay in the warmth of her embrace gripped him. He stepped back and took hold of her hands. He slowly nodded, let go of her, and stepped into the darkness.

CHAPTER SIXTEEN

France, 1918

The rain let up the first part of October, drying out the roads a bit. Even though there was a chill in the evening, the days were still warm. Rumors circulated that the Germans were close to collapsing. The malaise of war that Rose and everyone else had been living under for years seemed to finally be lifting. The first splashes of yellow and red spread across the woods to her right as Rose pedaled her bike up and over the small hill, crunching gravel under her tires. Past the white sandstone windmill, she bumped over the railroad tracks on the edge of the village. The streets were nearly deserted when she parked in front of Emil's Café. She preferred this establishment because it was an out-of-the-way place that her compatriots seemed to have overlooked, and English was rarely heard. It helped her forget the hospital, if only for a little while. On her rare days off, she liked to sit and drink tea and talk to the owners, Emil and Chantal, who fussed over her whenever she went in. The warm smell of fresh bread hit her as she opened the door, and the dinging bell announced her arrival.

A British soldier stood at the counter deep in conversation with Emil. He dressed the part of a Highlander with a navy-blue Glengarry bonnet and a khaki tunic over a dark green kilt. Her eyes followed the warp and weft of the green, white, and black threads of his tartan down to his well-developed calf muscles before realizing she was staring. The spell was broken by the sound of his Scottish burr assaulting the French language. Rose stifled a laugh as Emil looked to her for help.

"Perhaps I can be of assistance," she said. The soldier turned around. He had fair skin and warm brown eyes that were kind and inviting.

"I am afraid my French is not up to par. Could you be so kind? I'm trying to order tea and croissants."

Rose translated the man's order to Emil and placed her own as well.

Emil replied, "*Oui, Je comprends, maintenant.*"

The Scotsman removed his cap, revealing a closely cropped head of auburn hair. "Franklin Morrison, Lieutenant. I'm much obliged."

"Rose Maddox. It was no trouble."

"I'm not much good at languages. I've been in France for a year, and I still have a devil of a time with the lingo. You sound like a native."

"It's been three years for me. I've had a lot of practice."

When Emil emerged from behind the counter, Franklin said, "Would you care to join me?"

Before she could answer, Emil swept past them, setting the tray of tea and croissants on the table near the window where Rose normally sat. She shrugged, thinking, *What's the harm?* Franklin pulled out a chair for her and she gathered up her skirt to sit, patiently waiting for him to kick off the conversation.

"You're a nurse."

"Yes, I'm at the chateau up the road."

"I thought you looked familiar. I've been up there a few times; I've probably seen you before," he said.

"Probably."

He poured a spoonful of sugar in his tea and stirred it back and forth. "The end is near."

She laughed. "Are you always so morose?"

He chuckled. "I meant the war; it's coming to a close."

"Yes, not a moment too soon."

"What will you do, I mean, when you get home? Where is home if I may ask?"

"I grew up in the Lake District. And no, I don't know what I'll do. For a long time, I thought the war would never end. Now it seems like a dream." She took a bite of her croissant.

"What about you; where are you from?"

"I'm from Cromarty, near Inverness. My family owns a sheep farm. That's what I'll go back to."

"It's hard work. I know a little bit about farm life; my dad's a veterinarian."

"It's good for you. Makes a man out of you," he said with a wink.

Rose found his flirtatious behavior charming. He projected an easygoing confidence that served him well. A part of her was attracted to him, but another part was reluctant to take that leap of faith; it had taken her a long time to get over Sebastian. She had covered her heart for so long she thought it was simply not ready to begin again. They made small talk about the weather and what they missed most about home. She finished her tea and nudged the cup toward the middle of the table.

"I must be going. Thank you for your company. It was nice to meet you."

He stood as she pushed her chair back.

"Can I drive you? I've a lorry parked down the street."

"Thank you, but I'm on my bike."

"Oh, well good on you. Fine day for a ride. Perhaps I'll run into you at the hospital."

"I'll be the one in the nurse's uniform."

He laughed. "Yes, of course."

***

Franklin became a regular visitor at the hospital. He seemed to find the flimsiest of excuses to stop by, but she would make time, when possible, to sit and listen to his entertaining stories of farm life in the Highlands. During the second week of November, Franklin and two other junior officers showed up at the hospital. They each carried bottles of whiskey in their hands. Franklin shouted, "It's over, the Germans have surrendered!" Silence covered the ward, followed by low whispers. Rose and the others had been through so many false alarms and rumors of the war ending that no one wanted to take the bait. The smile on Franklin's face fell into a frown.

"What's that you say?" one of the orderlies yelled from the back of the room.

"It's over," he repeated. "An hour ago. I just heard the news."

The murmurs from the staff grew louder. Colonel Parker, the hospital director, burst into the room. Every pair of eyes in the room focused on his grinning face. "It's over, Germany has surrendered."

A cheer went up from one of the doctors, and the rest of the staff joined in. People hugged one another. Rose, having waited for this day for so long, was dumbfounded; the moment seemed unreal. She did not realize she was standing next to Eliza until she felt a hand on her shoulder.

Her friend's blue eyes filled with tears as they embraced. "It's really over; we're going home."

The colonel eyed the bottles of whiskey and turned to the nearest orderly. "Find some glasses; drinks are in order."

The bottles of Scotch made the rounds, and the Colonel led an impromptu version of "God Save the King." More whiskey was consumed, and people danced to "It's a Long Way to Tipperary" and "Let me call you Sweetheart." After her third drink—*or was it her fourth*—she found herself shuffling with Franklin in an awkward two-step. Intent on not getting her feet stepped on, she was looking down when he stopped. When she gazed up, an intensity in his eyes burned through her. The thought of being intimate with him had occurred to her, but she had tried to keep that image at arm's length to protect herself. Maybe it was the alcohol, maybe the passage of time, but now she wanted to let go of the ghosts that had haunted her for so long. He leaned in and kissed her, the sweet taste of whiskey on his soft lips. Her heart fluttered for a moment until she caught her breath. After a long several seconds, they broke apart and he grinned broadly as if partly embarrassed and partly proud. It surprised her how much she enjoyed the kiss, arousing something deep inside that she hadn't felt in a long time—a passion for living.

In the sober light of the next day, when her head stopped pounding, she chalked up the prior night's feelings to the whiskey. *This will not go any further*. Rose was both quietly relieved and regretful when Franklin's regiment rotated home a month later. Before he left, after some persistence on his part, she gave him her parents' address, and he promised to write.

CHAPTER SEVENTEEN

England, 1919

Rose returned to England in January. Living at her parents' house, she busied herself with volunteer work at the church and helping her father's practice. She drifted along, hardly noticing the passage of time, waiting for something to happen, a sign to tell her what to do. The flu virus went around, claiming Tommy and Mr. Kennerly. A few months after Rose came home, a letter arrived at her parents' house, postmarked Cromarty, Scotland. She stared at it for several seconds before tearing it open.

Dear Rose,

I hope this letter finds you safe and back in the loving embrace of your family. I can tell you that I am overjoyed to be back where my heart belongs, my majestic Highlands. Although I was only away for two years, I never realized how much this place means to me. The contrast between the trenches and the peacefulness of the mountains cannot be measured.

When I was away, I always thought of how beautiful this place was. I was afraid I might be disappointed when I returned, that it would not live up to my imagination. I couldn't have been more wrong. Yesterday, I took a rowboat out on the Firth to think about things. It had been one of those rare clear days that turned into a mild, soft evening when not a breath disturbs the air. The sun was setting, and the shades of evening were just starting to spread over the nearby hills, with thin vapors rising off the water. It was so peaceful and calm that I rested on the oars to take in the enchanting sight. The silence was broken by the sound of a choir practicing at the little stone church on the lakeshore. The windows must have been open, because I could clearly hear "Amazing Grace" floating through the gathering mist. It was the sweetest sound I ever heard. I wish you could have been here.

Enough of me bragging about the Highlands. I look forward to hearing about how you are getting on. Please write when you can. All the best.

Warmly,
Franklin

Rose held the letter in her hand and thought about writing back but stopped herself. What would I say to him? Tell him I'm at a loss as to how to get my life back on track. That day-to-day existence is small and unimportant after France. That everyone expects me to be normal; instead, I feel numb, as if the war has poisoned me. I should do him a favor and warn him that I'm going to end up crazy, like Mr. Kennerly. She quietly placed the envelope in the drawer of her secretary.

The letters came regularly for the next three months, one or two pages of Franklin telling her how beautiful the Highlands were, how busy they were on the farm, filling her in on the local happenings, and always asking her to write back. Rose never responded. When the letters stopped arriving, she ached with disappointment at the thought of what might have been.

On the first true day of summer, when the sun came up early and the morning seemed to last forever, Rose went on a hike with the dogs up to her meadow. She sat in the open field with the pups at her feet, trying to think of nothing. But she found herself recalling Franklin's letters, imagining how his voice sounded. The pall covering her heart slowly peeled away. A startling thought came to her; the last time she had been to her meadow was with Sebastian nearly five years earlier. A lifetime had passed since then.

Back at home, she sat at her secretary and picked up a paper and pen.

Dear Franklin,

I want to thank you for the wonderful letters you have sent me from the Highlands. It sounds like a delightful place. I must apologize for not responding earlier. I've not been myself lately and didn't think I was in the right frame of mind to write you back.

Before I went to France, I considered myself a happy person. I was on my way to becoming a nurse, and I was very much in love with a young man; I thought the world belonged to me. Fate intervened and we were pulled apart, so instead of the life I hoped for, I spent three years in the war. I saw the worst that humanity has to offer. I tried to put it all behind me when I returned home, but I can't. Sometimes at night, the sights and sounds of the dying men come back to visit me in my dreams. Sometimes, just a walk down a quiet country lane revives the image of row upon row of white crosses in the muddy French fields, leaving me without hope. I fear my experience in France has permanently damaged me. My sense of optimism died somewhere along the way.

I wanted you to know all of this as an explanation, not an excuse, for my poor correspondence. I wish you well and think of you often.

Warmly,
Rose

***

Franklin stared at the letter in his hand, a smile spreading across his broad face. He tore open the envelope. He read it silently at first, but eventually gave voice to the words. He didn't notice he was pacing until the blurred streaks on the windowpane came into focus. Outside, rain cascaded down on the sheep-covered hillside. He went to his bedroom and picked up his Bible from the nightstand. He thumbed through the pages until he found what he was looking for— Corinthians 13. Running his finger along the page, he repeated the words aloud. "Love bears all things, believes all things, hopes all things, endures all things." He put the Bible down, picked up his pen and wrote.

Dear Mr. Maddox,

My name is Franklin William Morrison. I am a friend of your daughter, Rose. We met in France at the end of the war. You may have noticed letters postmarked with my return address in Scotland. I've not had the chance to meet with you in person, but it is difficult for me to find time to get away from my obligations.

I am writing to ask for your daughter's hand in marriage. I realize you don't know me, so allow me this opportunity to tell you about myself. Until recently, I was an officer in His Majesty's army. I resigned my

*commission at the end of the war and returned to the
family farm, which I just inherited. The farm is quite
large and prosperous. It has been in the Morrison family
for several generations. We have been an integral part
of this community for centuries. I do not smoke, rarely
drink—and when I do, it is only the finest scotch
whiskey. I am a member of the Church of Scotland and
attend services every Sunday. My parents raised my
brothers and me to have faith in God, loyalty to the
Crown, and service to our country. Education was
sacrosanct. I intend to impart these same values to my
children.*

*Although I've only known Rose a short time, I very
much love your daughter and promise to provide her
with the good life she deserves. I understand that you
may be reluctant to grant such a request to a man
you've never met, and I will abide by whatever decision
you make. I respectfully await your response.*

*Sincerely,
Franklin W. Morrison*

***

Rose came home from one of her long walks and found
her father, on his afternoon off, sitting at the kitchen
table reading a letter. He quickly folded it, placed it in
the envelope, and put it in his jacket pocket. She thought
the postmark looked familiar.

James said, "Any word from your gentleman
correspondent?"

"No, I don't think he'll be writing back."

"Oh, I see." He frowned. "None of my business."

She ignored his feigned indifference. "I think I
discouraged him with my response. I wish I had replied
differently."

He shifted back in his chair. "Well, nothing that can't be put right with another letter. I'm sure if you explain yourself, he will understand."

"I was pretty blunt," she said, joining him at the table.

He placed his hand on top of hers until she raised her head and their eyes met. "Rose, he's seen you at your finest hour, a nurse serving in France. I'm sure he has a full picture of you."

"I don't know."

He pulled out his pipe and a packet of tobacco. "What kind of a man is he?"

"He's a good one. Well, he was nice to me. I know his family owns a large farm that keeps him busy."

Her father lit his pipe and shook the match out. "I've a friend who is a vet in North Ayrshire; he knows all the farmers there. I'll ring him up and get the full story."

"Oh, please don't bother."

"It's no bother at all."

Rose felt like she was up on a tightrope. She couldn't go back; she had to move forward, or she would fall.

***

Two weeks later, Rose sat at the kitchen table, having afternoon tea with her mother. The dogs jumped up as her father burst through the door holding a small bundle of mail in his left hand. The pups yipped and yapped as they followed him into the kitchen.

"I thought you had an errand to run," Rose said.

"I did. It didn't take as long as I thought. I picked up the mail while I was out. Oh, tea sounds lovely." Rose offered to get her father some. "I'll get it," he said, moving to the stove, patting his vest pocket. "Damn, I must have left my glasses in the car. Rose, could you be a dear and run out and get them. I need to read these bills."

"Of course." Her mother and father exchanged glances with one another as she slid her chair back and walked past the dogs through the surgery to the waiting room. Rose opened the door and thought her eyes were playing tricks on her. It was the first time she'd seen him out of uniform, but she would have recognized him anywhere. Franklin Morrison, in a navy-blue single-breasted waistcoat and white wing-collared shirt, stood in the front yard.

"Oh, my Lord!" she gasped.

He smiled at her, holding a bouquet of flowers in one hand, removing his hat with the other. She shut the door behind her, anxious that her parents might see this.

"Franklin, what are you doing here? How did you get here?"

"Your father picked me up at the station."

"He did?" The words were clear but didn't make sense and only raised more questions. The pieces slowly began to fall into place, the letter quickly secreted away, her father's errand-run, the exchange of glances—they'd arranged this. They're probably watching from the window right now, she thought. Her face flushed hot with embarrassment.

Before she could utter another word, Franklin held the flowers out. "These are for you," he said, placing his hat back on his head. He pulled a small black box from the pocket of his waistcoat, held it out, and lifted the lid. Inside was an antique ring.

Franklin cleared his throat. "This was my grandmother's wedding ring." He took a deep breath, got down on one knee and looked up at her. "I love you, Rose, and I'll always be here for you. I know you've been struggling, that you're hurting and want to guard your heart. Know that I will love you no matter what. I'm asking you for your hand in marriage today and to trust that God will grant us a tomorrow. Will you have me as your husband?"

Rose was dumbstruck. "I … I … I …" She felt as if she were standing outside of herself looking down at this small moment playing out on the stone walkway to her parent's house. Her heart unfurled, and a thousand thoughts raced through her head. She wanted him to kiss her and take her in his arms. For the first time in a long time, she saw hope and love shimmering before her. The word that came out of her mouth sounded like it was being spoken by an actress in a play.

"Yes."

"You will?"

"Yes!"

He stood and opened his arms to her. She took a hesitant step forward, then made a leap of faith and flung herself into them. His arms came tight around her, crushing her in his embrace. Rose buried her face in his neck and knew that, for the first time in a long time, she was home.

EPILOGUE

Northeastern France, 1954

Rose parked the rental car in the gravel lot separating the country lane from the perimeter of the cemetery. She rechecked the directions that had been given to her, retracing her lefts and rights through the Alsatian villages of Pechelbronn and Kutzenhausen. "This must be the place," she said to no one, switching off the engine. A buzz of voices came through the open window. Up ahead in the village proper, a crowd gathered. The white and brown of the timber and stone houses acted as a canvas for the villagers. The women wore long sleeve cotton blouses, and big black skirts coming down over their knees. The men wore cotton shirts with red waistcoats and black felt hats. The women's bonnets looked like elephant's ears, but she thought they framed their faces perfectly. She guessed it must be part of a celebration, probably a wedding. The joy and excitement of the crowd touched her as she remembered her own wedding. She wondered how many friends' and family members' lives intersected today.

Summer's heat clung to her as she stepped into the

still afternoon air. Rose shrugged off her jacket, smoothing her skirt before retrieving the bouquet of flowers from the passenger seat. Cars and trucks streamed past into the village. She pushed open the wrought iron gate that separated the land of the dead from the land of the living. The flowers were for her friend Eliza's son Duncan, an RAF flier whose bomber had been shot down over France. Rose had offered to visit his grave while she and Franklin were on holiday in the region. Back in Scotland, it all seemed remote, an afterthought at the time. Here, the gravity of the situation weighed on her. She had to pause before continuing.

She remembered Duncan in his RAF Blues, and her son James in his heather-colored kit, both with their caps jauntily cocked to one side, serenading the party with Christmas carols. They seemed immortal, full of vitality, like the gods had dipped them in a protective coating to ward off evil. A wave of melancholy washed over her, reliving the pain of having someone you love ripped away. You spend the rest of your life caressing the contours of a wound that never heals, she thought.

"Do you need some help?" came a voice in French.

A tall man with liquid brown eyes stood several paces away. He wore the black pants, white shirt, and red waistcoat that the other villagers wore. Something about him was familiar, but she couldn't put her finger on it. Rose carefully composed her response.

"Yes. I'm searching for the graves of the British airmen," she replied in her best French.

The man paused, making her wonder if her syntax was incorrect. He responded in American accented English. "You are British?"

"Yes, are you American?"

"I'm originally from here, but I live in America now.

Let me show you where they're at."

Poplar trees lined the southern and eastern flanks of the cemetery. They walked through rows of stone markers, some modest slabs of granite, others more ornate crypts. Soldiers killed in both World Wars. The names of the deceased were German but many of the inscriptions were in French. The young man led her to the edge of the cemetery where simple crosses were paired with Union Jacks. A plaque, in French and English, stood next to the flag on the end. She read in a soft voice, "To the memory of five British airmen whose plane crashed near the village of Kutzenhausen: McKenzie, Duncan, Sgt." There it was—the first name on the list. A pang of sadness tugged at her, and her voice caught. She wished Franklin were here to lean on. Embarrassed to show any emotion in front of a total stranger, she read the other names in a steady voice. The young man cleared his throat.

"If I may ask, are you related to any of these men?"

"No, it's for a friend back home. Duncan McKenzie is her son. I've known him since he was a baby. I told her I would visit his grave while we were on holiday in the area. It's the least I could do."

"You're a good friend. Are you traveling alone?"

"No, my husband is with me. But he was not feeling well this morning. He's back at the hotel in Wissembourg."

"I see. I don't mean to intrude. I'll leave you now."

Rose watched him walk away. The cemetery, although modest in appearance, was immaculately clean. Many of the graves had small plaques laid out next to the tombstones, expressing final sentiments to grandmothers, fathers, aunts, or uncles. She wondered how many lives these people touched. Some of those touched were no doubt standing in the village square right now. Duncan fell to earth in this place and was now a part of the fabric of their lives, forever a part of their history. She would make sure to convey to Eliza that her son's grave was well looked after.

She thought about the cruel irony of life. Eliza and her husband Bert, two of the most decent people she knew, lost their only son to the war. Rose's son, James, came home from his stint with the Highlanders unscathed, physically at least. Jamie never talked about his experiences, but she had been around enough soldiers, and knew her son well enough, to recognize he was hiding his pain. He would never again hit the high notes in life, not like before the war. She understood that feeling all too well.

She laid the bouquet down and turned to go. The man who had helped her sat on a concrete bench under the shade of a poplar tree on the opposite side of the cemetery. She thought about waving goodbye as she made her exit, but relished the opportunity to speak English, if only for a moment. Serving as a translator for her linguistically challenged husband had become wearisome. She threaded her way between the rows of stones. He smiled at her approach, putting her at ease.

"Thank you for your help, it was nice to speak English for a change."

"My pleasure," he replied.

"If you don't mind my asking, what is everybody dressed up for?"

"There's a wedding."

"That's what I figured. A friend of yours, family?"

He blushed. "Actually, it's my wedding."

She laughed. "Congratulations. Are you hiding out because you have second thoughts?"

He chuckled. "No, no. This is the first time I've been back to Alsace in many years. It's my first visit to my father's grave."

Her light banter felt silly now, an intrusion on someone else's private affair. She looked away from the young man to the marker before him.

Sebastian Maier 06/08/1894 -21/07/1951.

The hairs on the back of her neck raised. Her skin turned to gooseflesh. Her brain couldn't put it all together, couldn't connect the etching in the granite with the name burnished in her memory. But her heart pounded out a message, thumping against her ribs until the brain caught up. *It's him.* Her knees felt weak, her face became warm. *It's him.* The man was up in an instant, taking her by the hand, leading her to the bench.

"You're not well," he said, with an edge of concern in his voice.

She held on to him, drawing in deep breaths. Her heart slowly calmed down, breathing became regular, and the fuzzy feeling in her head lifted.

"You look like you've seen a ghost."

"I have," she replied.

The puzzled look on his face told her she'd have to tell her story now, if only to hear the rest of Sebastian's story. He sat on the bench next to her.

"I knew your father."

"How?"

"Before the war, in England." She told him how they had met, how the war pulled them apart. The young man listened patiently. She wondered at the appropriateness of this disclosure. If she was lucky, he would quietly dismiss her, and she could retreat with her dignity intact.

"You're Rose."

"You know who I am?"

"He showed me your photo. You look remarkably unchanged."

The sound of her name, delivered by a stranger in a

familiar tone, hit her ears like a dissonant note. She never discussed her relationship with Sebastian with anyone other than her parents. After their stilted reunion, it was easier not to think about it. She didn't know what happened to him after they last parted. Part of her was scared to find out that he might have been killed or maimed. Decorum would have precluded the question that followed, but curiosity got to her first.

"What did he say about me?"

Now it was the young man's turn to draw in deeply, pausing before sighing. "When I had the opportunity to go to America, I was filled with doubts about leaving my family and friends. I had been away in the army for a long time and didn't want to leave Alsace again. Papa convinced me to go. He said I'd rue not going. He told me his only regret in life was a girl he met in England. He was in love and was going to ask her to marry him; he even put down a payment on a ring." The man gazed in the distance, as if searching for something. "But then came the war, closing that chapter forever."

She willed her heart to beat slowly as tears spilled down her cheeks. Many nights in France she'd relived their moments together, analyzing every little thing Sebastian said, trying to determine how deep was his love. As the years progressed, she convinced herself that their time together was just a phase, and it was silly to think they could have had a future together. Now, filled with the knowledge that the lottery of fate had canceled their future, her tears tasted bittersweet. The young man paused to hand her his handkerchief.

"I'm sorry," she said. "I'm normally not like this."

"No need to apologize," he said, as she dabbed her eyes.

"Was he happy?" she asked.

"He was a good husband, a good father. I think the

war haunted him. He tried to keep it at bay."

She didn't want the conversation to end. Talking about Sebastian stirred up ghosts for her, the words like a memory she wanted to savor.

"We did meet again. Your father and I."

He arched his eyebrows at her. "When?"

Rose explained their meeting at the hospital and the letter he gave her. "It was awkward. British nurse, German soldier, not well received, as you can imagine." She breathed a long, slow breath. "It was worth it. Seeing him again, after wondering for so long, it revived me. Before our reunion, I'd been sad because of what I'd lost. After our rendezvous, after the shock wore off, I learned to be happy for the good times we'd had. At least, I tried to be." More cars streamed into the village. The buzz of voices had become a swarm. She wondered if she looked like a foolish old woman, unburdening herself to a stranger. The young man's eyes shone with a keen interest that dampened her worries. Enough, she told herself, remember your manners. "I don't mean to take up your time. You should return to your party."

He laughed. "You're right. No wedding without a groom."

"I don't know your name."

"Paul."

Sparrows, hidden in the junipers, serenaded them out of the cemetery. He walked her to the car, holding the door open and shaking her hand before she settled in the seat.

"I'm glad to have met you," he said.

She suddenly remembered the amulet and asked Paul about it. He reached under his collar and pulled it out.

"I have it right here. I wore it during the war. My mother thought it would bring me luck." He glanced down at it. "I guess she was right." He tucked the icon back under his collar. "*Au revoir*."

"*Au revoir*," she replied. He started for the village square. Instead of turning the engine over, she watched him striding confidently toward the church spires that rose above the neighboring houses. When he reached the edge of the crowd, cheering and clapping went up.

The End

Thank you for reading my book. I would greatly appreciate it if you left a review. A review is a great opportunity to provide feedback that allows me to serve my readers better. You can leave a review on Amazon.com or goodreads.com/garybaysingerauthor.

Nothing fancy, just a few honest words.

Acknowledgements

This novel is a labor of love. It started as the middle section of another book, but after overthinking things, I thought it might make a stand-alone story. If you have seen my website, you'll know that the genesis for this book was a scene from a movie called *Oh! What a Lovely War*. I set the book in Yorkshire because I lived there as a teenager and I love James Heriot.

I received a lot of help along the way. My eternal gratitude to my wife Carrie, son Noah, and sister Amy, for taking the time to read my work and give me feedback. None of this would have been possible without the input from my writer's group: Natalie, Jim, Warren, Marilyn, Mike, Dave, Tonya, EW, Jessica, and Lisa. Thanks to Kim for the marketing advice and thanks to Jeff for walking me through the cover process. Many thanks to my editors Pam and Louise for helping to get things just right.

About the cover

When I was researching the book, I needed to know what a World War One nurse's uniform looked like. Through the magic of the internet, I found the image you see on the front cover. I did not give much thought to the young lady in the photo, I was more interested in her uniform. Much later, I came across the image again and discovered there was a story behind the woman in the photo. Her name is Violet Jessop. She was a steward on the British ocean liner *RMS Olympic*. She was onboard the ship in September 1911, when the Olympic collided with a British warship. Despite extensive damage, the ship returned to port without sinking. In April 1912, Violet transferred to the *Titanic*. She was one of seven hundred people to survive. When war broke out in 1914, Violet volunteered as a nurse on the hospital ship, *Britannic*. In November 1916, the *Britannic* struck a mine while sailing in the Aegean Sea. While the ship was sinking, Violet had to abandon her lifeboat to avoid being shredded by the ship's propellers. Violet returned to work as a steward in 1920. She died in 1971 at the age of eighty-three

Below is an excerpt from my novel, *"Margaret's Last Prayer"*

Available on Amazon

Alsace, 1924

The first time he'd dreamed this dream, Sebastian Maier was grateful he didn't disturb his wife Yvette and their infant son Paul as they lay sleeping next to him. The images stayed with him for days as he tried to decipher the meaning. He'd had dreams about the Great War before, most of them he'd tried to forget. As chilling as this one was, it didn't seem to have anything to do with him. It felt familiar, as if a faint cloud of déjà vu amplified its significance. It was like an answer was right in front of him, but he didn't know what the question was.

In the dream, he stood on the banks of a river watching a long grey line of soldiers shimmy and slither across a damaged bridge that spanned a river he didn't recognize. The gray-green uniforms of the men crossing the bridge looked German to him. The soldiers waiting to receive their surrender wore short khaki-colored jackets with yellow and blue shoulder patches. Their helmets were rounded and oblong, unlike the flat tin pots the Americans and British wore. Sebastian thought they might be a French colonial regiment, but as he wandered among them, he heard English spoken, in a drawl that was different from the English he learned in his time in England before the war. He guessed they were American.

The Germans staggered up the bank, appearing relieved as they discarded their rifles onto the huge pile of weapons accumulating where the road met the bridge. The captors shouted, "*Hande Hocht*!" and began searching the prisoners.

Sebastian stood next to an American, whose wiry build and bright blue eyes reminded him of his father, Walter. The American took short, sharp breaths, staring hard at the prisoners, anger seething out of him, seemingly on edge. He lashed out at a passing German, striking him in the back. He kicked at another soldier. Both prisoners scurried away to avoid the American soldier's wrath. The man seemed like a wrecking ball cut loose from its chain, looking to destroy something or someone. A third prisoner, as tall as Sebastian but with a more solid build, approached. The man looked eerily like the photo Sebastian had seen of his wife Yvette's brother, Paul, the one who'd been killed in the trenches at Ypres, the one she named their son after. His ruminations were interrupted when the American smacked the young man's head, knocking off his cap, revealing a shock of dark hair. Instead of retreating, the prisoner turned and faced his attacker. The American's face went red, his right hand went to the pistol on his hip as he grabbed the German by his tunic with the left hand.

He's going to shoot him. Sebastian grabbed at the gun in the soldier's hand, holding tight to prevent the gun from being freed. The American relaxed his grip, the rage in his eyes subsiding as he stared straight ahead. Sebastian followed the American's gaze. The prisoner wore an amulet around his neck. It was not unusual for a soldier to wear a religious icon for good luck. This one shocked him with its familiarity —a cross, set inside a heart, laid inside a rose. Sebastian's amulet: the one that had been in the Maier family for over a hundred years, the one he'd worn during the Great War. He looked into the German soldier's eyes. The resemblance to Paul, the brother-in-law he never knew, astonished him. "Who are you?" he asked.

About the author: Gary Baysinger

Gary loves a good story. He spent his formative years on the site of a World War Two battlefield, where he shook hands with a king and a president. Inspired by comic books and Hollywood cinema, he married his interest in military history with Ancestry.com to re-imagine the family tree as an outline for a story. He is a direct descendant of Margaret Laemmer from his novel, "*Margaret's Last Prayer.*" He is a graduate of the University of Baltimore and a veteran of the U.S. Coast Guard. Gary began writing in 2016 and lives in Milwaukie, Oregon with his wife, two children, and two dogs.

Check out books, author interviews, and music at: **Garybaysingerauthor.com**. I am on facebook at Garybaysingerauthor.

I also make a cameo appearance on COPS as the shirtless, intoxicated man, lecturing the authorities on what constitutes a reasonable search and seizure.

Printed in Great Britain
by Amazon

26220440R00078